Mr Anthony
of
Ballygullion

Also by Lynn Doyle

Ballygullion

'The wit, the ear for dialect and the sheer gusto of the telling exercise an unfading charm.'

The Irish Press

Mr Anthony
of
Ballygullion

Lynn Doyle

Blackstaff Press

Published by Blackstaff Press, 3 Galway Park, Dundonald, Belfast BT16 0AN.

ISBN 0 85640 207 9

Printed in Northern Ireland by Excel Printing Services Limited.

Contents

The stories in this book were originally published as follows: 'A Wild Goose Chase' in *Lobster Salad* (Duckworth, 1922); 'Sense and Sawdust' in *Me and Mr Murphy* (Duckworth, 1930); 'A Sweepstake' and 'A Wag of a Tail' in *Rosabelle and other stories* (Duckworth, 1933); 'Dear Ducks' and 'Sealing Wax' in *Dear Ducks and other 'Ballygullion' Stories* (Duckworth, 1925), and 'Turkey and Ham' in *The Shake of the Bag* (Duckworth, 1939).

A Wild-Goose Chase

Havin' a taste for a thing and bein' able to do it isn't altogether the same, though there's some people thinks it is.

An' wee Mr Anthony the solicitor was wan av thim. He had the terriblest notion av all kinds av sport av any man I ever knowed, an' in particular av shootin'; an' he was a bigger dunderhead at shootin' than he was at anythin' else, an' that, mind ye, is saying a good deal.

If it hadn't been that he was always at the safe end av the gun there'd ha' been a Crowner's jury sittin' on himself before he ever seen twenty-five; an' if there hasn't been wan sittin' on some av his friends up till now, it's only puttin' it off.

Everything else, fish, flesh, and fowl, he'd shot some time or another, down to the tin weather-cock on Tammas Dorrian's barn, that he took for a wood-pigeon, an' never knowed to the differs till he heard the jingle av it on the slates.

In the first place, he was a wee, nervous, twittery kind av a man, with his hands always ready to shoot a couple av seconds or so before his head was, an' in the next, he was as short-sighted as a ten-days-old pup.

Not that that would ha' mattered if he'd put on glasses like another body — my ould grandfather wore specs an' could ha' shot snipe till he was seventy — but Mr Anthony was a natty, dressy wee body, an' would wear divil a thing but an eyeglass; an' half his time he was either unwindin' the string av it from round the barrels av the gun, or pickin' bits av the glass out av the breech.

Eye-glasses must ha' come heavy on him. He always carried a stock av thim with him. I remember him using up three in one while av an afthernoon, an' divil a' all he shot in the end but a setter pup that the mercy av Providence sent between my legs an' him when the gun went off.

So though he was mortial fine pay, an' the best av good company, he was no great shootin' companion for a man with a young family; an' when he come into my yard with the gun in his hand a couple av days afther he shot the pup, I'd very near as soon ha' seen the ould Fellow himself.

But there wasn't a bit av use av me tryin' to put him off.

'Now, Pat,' sez he, 'ye'll have to come, that's all about it. Wee Sonny Burke came into Ballygullion this afthernoon on an errand to tell me there's a flock av wild geese in Miss Armytage's bog; an' I might never have a chance like it in my life again. I never shot a wild goose yet,' sez he, all fidgetin'.

'No,' sez I, 'an' ye never shot a tenant-farmer yet, but you're goin' to do it now if ye don't stop footherin' with that gun. For mercy sake put it down on the ditch there till I talk to ye. Don't ye know there hasn't been a shot fired in Miss Armytage's demesne these two years an' more.'

An' that was true enough.

Ould Miss Armytage was one av thim ould ladies that never havin' got a man or a child av her own to turn their kindliness an' good-heartedness on, was always squandherin' them on somethin' else that hadn't the same need av them.

Many's the thing she took up wi' from the time she lost all hope; dogs an' cats, an pigs, an' the heathen — at home an' at Ballygullion; but at the time I spake av she was all for kindness to animals in general.

Not a finger dare ye lay on a livin' thing about the place. The pheasants an' partridges was as thick as sparrows, an' the country for a mile round the demesne fair polluted wi' rabbits; but the divil a trigger would she let be drawn where she had any say.

And about the Big House itself it was worse than all. Every hen an' duck in the yard had its name on a wee brass ring round its leg, an' knowed its name too, an' would come when it was called by it; but if the whole household was starvin' ye daren't put a knife on one av their throats. The best cook ever she had she sacked at a minit's notice for killin' an' servin' up a young pullet called Emily Ann one day the District Inspector turned up unexpected for lunch; forbye that she held a burial service over the bird, an' put up a headstone to it in the back garden.

The yardman had an extra five shillin's for everybody he caught killin' flesh or fowl about the house an' grounds, an' each av the gamekeepers the same for every poacher he caught; so that between one thing an' another, to walk across an acre av Miss Armytage's land was as good as layin' down forty shillin's an' costs; keepin' off the disgrace av bein' up before the Bench.

I put all this before Mr Anthony, an' more to the back av it; but I might as well ha' saved my breath; for he was an obstinate as a he-ass when he had his mind made up about a thing. He was out to shoot a wild goose, an' a wild goose he would shoot, an' all the good I did by talkin' was to make him that nervous av bein' caught that he fetched me over four barbed-wire fences an' a march-drain instead av goin' into the demesne by the road. An' if it did lift my heart a bit to see him leave the seat av his new shootin' breeches on the first wire-fence, I fell into the drain myself an' got a cold that nearly brought me to my grave.

We were pushin' along the edge av the wee wood that lay between us an' the marsh, Mr Anthony leadin' the way, wi' both barrels cocked, though the wather was a quarther av a mile off yet, when all at once he jukes down behind the stump av a tree.

'Wheesht, Pat,' sez he. 'I see a rabbit on the path in front of us — not eighty yards away. I'll have a shot at it. It'll get my eye in.'

'Will ye be wise?' sez I. 'Isn't it bad enough runnin' the risk av a shot in the marsh without firin' wan here, where we're as near again to the Big House.'

'Hang the Big House,' sez he, all in a flurry; 'we're not within half a mile av it. An' I never seen a rabbit sittin' betther for a shot. I couldn't miss it if I tried. It's away,' sez he, all disappointed, peepin' over the stump. 'Wait, it's not, I see it. But it's farther off than I thought; stay you here, an' I'll double in among the trees.'

An' away he goes, stalkin' in an' out, an' crouchin' an' crawlin', till he'd taken the price av half a dozen rabbits out av the remains av the shooting suit. The divil av a rabbit could I see; an' presently Mr Anthony straightens himself an' steps out into the path again. When I got up to him he was rubbin' the eyeglass on a piece av shammy leather, an' swearing most lamentable.

'What was it, Mr Anthony?' sez I. 'Is it gone?'

'A most extraordinary thing, Pat,' sez he, lookin' a bit foolish, an' rubbin' away like fury wi' the shammy. 'I'll be blest,' sez he, 'if it wasn't a bit av hayseed on my eyeglass all the time. I'd have taken my oath it was a rabbit. I saw the scut an' the two ears as plain as I see you. If ye laugh, ye ould scoundrel,' sez he, 'I'll put the two barrels in ye.'

'Is it laugh at ye, Mr Anthony?' sez I. 'I wouldn't think av such a thing.' An' the next minit I was holdin' on to a tree an' laughin' till I lost my breath.

I'd ha' been laughin' yet, I believe, between the fun av the thing an' the look av Mr Anthony, but just as I was in the middle av a kink there comes a whistle from up the path in front av us.

'By the Lord Harry, it's a gamekeeper,' sez Mr Anthony. 'Quick, Pat!' He grabbed the gun by the muzzle, an' stuck her well into a bunch av briers, an' the two av us down behind the briers on our hands an' knees.

Sure enough, it was Long James, the head gamekeeper. He passed us that close he could ha' touched us. I suppose, to a man like a solicitor, brought up in the middle av them, an oath or two isn't the same as to another body; but there's no doubt that when Mr Anthony was in a tight place he swore like a baliff's officer.

'In the name av goodness, Mr Anthony,' sez I, 'will ye stop swearin'? Sure, the man's clean gone, an' no harm done.'

'Bad luck to him again for a long string av misery,' sez Mr Anthony, still muttherin' as he riz from his knees: 'what brought him round this way? He has me all in a twitter. Come here, you,' sez he, very vicious—takin' a pluck at the gun by the muzzle.

An' wi' that bang goes the right barrel. When the smoke riz, an' I looked for the bits av Mr Anthony; he was standin' there thrimmlin', as white as a ghost, an' lookin' a kind av a stupid way at the tails av his coat, that was all chattered wi' the shot.

'Did ye see that, Pat?' was all he could get out. 'Did ye see that? I ruined my breeches on that infernal wire fence, an' now there's the coat gone too.'

'Never mind your coat, Mr Anthony,' sez I, snappin' up the gun. 'Long James'll be back on the top av us.' We could hear the shouts av him comin'.

'Make for the crown av the wood,' sez I, as we ran. 'We can hide in the bracken.'

I never seen Mr Anthony run like it. If the eyeglass hadn't lapped round an ash saplin' an' fetched him up with a jerk that near sthrangled him, I'd ha' never caught up with him till he was in the middle av the marsh.

'Are we safe, Pat?' sez he, gaspin', on his face in the bracken. 'Are we clean away from the rascal? I wouldn't for ten pound he'd get a catch at me. I beat him in a poachin' case at the last sessions, an' he's had it in for me ever since.'

'This is all Brown the gunsmith's fault,' sez he, gettin' savager as he found his breath, 'the clumsy, brainless ould fool. First he had the gun pullin' off that stiff that I shot Joe Nevin's ferret, an' me aimin' at a rabbit ten yards to the left av it; an' now he has her that light that she'd go off if ye blew your breath on her. If I'd been pullin' her wi' the muzzle towards me just now I'd have had an action again him.'

'If ye'd been pullin' wi' the muzzle towards you, Mr Anthony,' sez I, 'ye'd never have throubled the law courts again, barrin' the takin' out av probate on your will. It's on your knees ye should be, givin' thanks that you're alive, instead av lyin' there cursin' an innocent man that had no more to do with it than I have. Long James must ha' missed us,' sez I. 'Gather up that gun an' come on home out av this.'

'Gimme her,' sez he, sittin' up an' screwin' in the eyeglass very determined. 'Ye can please yourself, Pat; but out av this demesne I don't go till I get a shot at them wild geese.'

'Ye'll be here then till the last trumpet frightens them away,' sez I, 'for ye wouldn't hit a wild goose till the Day av Judgment wi' the state av nerves you're in now.'

But no, he wouldn't give in. His blood was up all the more wi' the vexation, an' the fright he'd got. I kept him arguin' there till I thought the gamekeeper would be gone home, an' then for peace sake I settled with him that he'd have wan shot an' no more. After that we were to go home, goose or no goose. For, thinks I, he's sure to let the gun off at the first tuft av rushes he sees, an' then we'll be away out av this as hard as we can.

But luck wouldn't have it that way. We weren't right at the edge av the marsh till, sure enough, half a dozen geese dashes out av the rushes. Bang goes Mr Anthony; there was a terrible splashin' in the wather, an' when the smoke riz there was a goose scutterin' here and there on the surface av the bog-hole with a broken wing.

Mr Anthony gives wan wild yell av delight, an' into the marsh. It never come into his head to fire the other barrel an' shoot the goose outright; but he grabs the gun near the muzzle wi' both hands, an' runs round the edge av the bog-hole thryin' to brain the bird with the butt.

Och, ye should ha' seen the spangs av him round that bog-hole, trippin' over tussocks av rushes, an' stumblin' in an' out av wee side drains, cursin' and thrashin' away at the goose, an' all the time callin' on me to help him. If I hadn't run up as quick as I could wi' the laughin' and whished the goose over towards him, the second barrel would ha' been out through his backbone, sure. He aimed a most lamentable blow at the goose as it come within range, an' more by good luck than good guidin' put it out av its pain with a dunt on the head would ha' felled an ox. The next minit he had it by the neck, an' was dancin' on the edge like a madman, shoutin' an' wavin' it round his head.

'For the love av goodness, Mr Anthony,' sez I, 'keep quiet and make for the wood, or every gamekeeper in the demesne'll be down on us. There's Long James!' sez I. 'Run!'

I was only makin' that up, but it sobered him; an' he made for the wood like a lamplighter, the gun in wan hand an' the goose in the other.

When I caught up with him he was lyin' in the bracken admiring the dead goose.

'Did ye ever see a finer goose in your life, Pat?' sez he all excited. 'Isn't it a beauty? An' as fat as mud. Feel the breast av it.'

I took the bird in my hand. 'It looks very big for a wild goose,' sez I.

'What do you mean?' sez Mr Anthony.

He took a hard look at the goose. His jaw fell. I could see the red risin' in his face. 'Ye don't mean to say —' sez he, stammerin'. He looked at the bird again.

'Pat,' sez he, in a kind av a whisper. 'Pat. There's somethin' on its leg.'

I looked. Round the right leg av the goose was a wee brass ring.

'There's writin' on it, Mr Anthony,' sez I. 'What does it say?'

'It looks like a name,' sez he, puttin' the glass in his eye. 'Blast me, but it looks like a name. It *is* a name,' sez he — '"Algernon Charles".'

'Oh, Mr Anthony dear,' sez I, 'ye'll be the death av me. Ye've shot Miss Armytage's prize gander that she named afther her uncle, the ould Major.'

Mr Anthony never said a world, but riz up an' walked away behind a wee clump av bushes. I could hear him holdin' a very bitther argument with himself an' gettin' a deal the worst av it.

Presently he come back, a bit quietened down, but still very vicious-lookin'.

'Curse the bird,' sez he, lookin' at it. 'It serves it right. Sure it flew. You saw it, Pat. What the divil made a tame gander fly, anyway?'

'The same thing as brought us here, Mr Anthony,' sez I, 'want av sense. Hide it in the bracken, an' come on home. Nobody'll be a bit the wiser.'

'I'll hide none av it in the bracken,' sez he, settin' his teeth. 'I killed it,' sez he, 'an' I'll eat it, if it was only for spite.'

'Have a bit av wisdom, Mr Anthony,' sez I. 'Sure ye can't walk home in broad daylight carryin' wan av Miss Armytage's tame geese. If it came out on ye, she'd have ye struck off the rolls.'

'Tie the legs round my neck,' sez he, 'an' let it hang down undher my coat. Nobody'll notice it from a distance, an' if I was the length av your house, I'll wait there till dark.'

'Ye couldn't do it,' sez I. 'Sure the neck would be hanging below your knees.'

'Well, you take it, Pat,' sez he. 'You're taller than I am.'

'Divil a fear av me,' sez I. 'If I'm taller I have more wit. An' if anybody's goin' to jail over this job, it'll be the man that fired the shot. But if ye're wise, ye'll leave it here. Ye'll have no luck over it. Wait till ye see.'

An' it turned out the way I said. Just as we were well into the back road out av the demesne, round the corner comes Ruddell, the huntsman, an' the whole pack av staghounds.

The two av us were over the ditch in a crack.

'Lie down, Mr Anthony,' sez I, crouchin' behind a bush. 'Lie down or he'll see you.'

'Divil a bit av me'll lie down,' sez Mr Anthony. 'We're out av the demesne land. I'll keep my face to him, an' he'll see nothin' but the gun.'

'He'll see the feet av the gander undher your chin,' sez I.

'It makes no odds,' sez Mr Anthony. 'He'll think it's a breastpin. I near blew the intestines out av myself for a gamekeeper the day already, an' I'll not risk my life for a huntsman.'

'A fine day, huntsman,' he shouts, as the pack went past.

The huntsman touched his hat an' rode on, never noticin' anythin'.

'Now, ye ould fool,' sez Mr Anthony, as we walked along the road, 'didn't I tell ye it would be all right? An' that's an *alibi* established. The huntsman seen me at four o'clock, an' I had no goose in my possession. For an ould sportsman, Pat, ye have little gumption. Now we're well out av it all, whatever happens. What's that behind us, Pat?' sez he suddenly.'Oh, it's only a stragglin' hound. Go home, ye brute,' sez he, 'ye frightened me.'

But the dog had no notion av going home. We weren't ten yards further till he was sniffin' at Mr Anthony's heels again.

'What the deuce does the animal want?' sez Mr Anthony. 'Go home, sir.'

'He must smell the gander,' sez I. An' with that the dog bones the bird by the neck.

'Ah, ye brute!' sez Mr Anthony; 'let go, let go this minit.'

But the dog didn't let go. Instead av that he took a fresh hold, an' near lit Mr Anthony on his back.

'Confound the dog,' sez Mr Anthony, in a rage. 'I'll murdher him. Chew, sir, chew!' An' he lashes behind him wi' the gun.

'Easy with the gun, Mr Anthony,' sez I. 'Ye know what happened the day already.' But I was too late. There was a flash an' a bang an' the next minit the dog was kickin' in his death-thraw in the middle av the road.

For a minit the two av us stood lookin' at him, dumbfoundhered.

'May the divil fly away with ould Brown, the gunsmith,' sez Mr Anthony at last, in a kind of lament. 'He's goin' to be the ruin av my whole career. This is dreadful — dreadful. If I'm not struck off the rolls,I'll be laughed out av the profession anyway. What'll I do now, at all, at all?'

'If ye could get the divil to fly away wi' the gander an' the dog, Mr Anthony,' sez I, 'it would be more to the purpose. Ruddell'll be back any minit, looking' for the hound, an' he'll see the two av them, an' then you an' I may lave the counthry. What are we goin' to do with them?'

'To the divil with both av them,' sez Mr Anthony, in a dancin' rage all at once. 'I'll show ye what I'll do. Here,' sez he — he cut the gander free av his neck, an' took the bird by the legs — 'away you to blazes,' an' he pitched it as far as he could over the hedge. 'Fly now, blast ye,' sez he; 'ye could fly when ye weren't wanted to. An' go you afther it,' sez he, staggerin' over to the ditch with the body av the dog. 'Worry the goose now, if ye can,' sez he, 'an' the divil choke ye on it. An' to pot wi' you as well,' sez he, 'it was you got me into all the bother, you an' the ould fool av a gunsmith that begot ye.' An' before I could say a word the gun went spinnin' over the ditch too, an' away goes Mr Anthony down the road, fair foamin'.

'Mr Anthony,' sez I, runnin' afther him, 'Mr Anthony, show some kind av sense. Ye might as well give yourself up at once. Sure, your name's on the breech av the gun.'

He stopped dead, an' looked at me with his mouth open.

'Away for the gun, Pat,' sez he, at the last, 'an' blow out my brains with it. No,' sez he, 'no, I have no brains. I'm not fit to be trusted out by myself. Take me home, an' put me to bed.'

'We'll have to hide the dog, Mr Anthony,' sez I. 'Sure, Ruddell seen ye with the gun, an' he'll put two an' two together. Wait, an' I'll hide him in the sally-bushes over yonder, an' then we'll go the length av my house for a spade an' bury him. We'll ha' time enough. Ruddell'll never miss him till he gets to the kennel. Will I bring ye the gander?'

'No,' sez Mr Anthony, breakin' out again, 'bring me no gander. Bury it,' sez he, 'an' bury the gun — an' bury me too, if ye like, for there's neither luck nor grace about me. Come on, Pat. I'm away for the spade. There's no time to be lost.'

It was wearin' on to dusk when we got back.

'Now, Mr Anthony,' sez I, 'you keep watch on the road here, an' I'll go an' bury the dog on this side av the sally-bushes. The gander is well enough hid in the rushes where he is.'

'Is it me keep watch?' sez he. 'The whole hunt might be on top av us before I'd see them. Gimme the spade,' sez he, 'an' you look out. I can handle a spade as well as a gun, I'd have ye know,' sez he, seein' me lookin' at him.

'An' troth,' sez I to meself, 'if ye can handle it no betther the huntsman'll catch us yet.' But it was true what he said about the watchin', so I let him go.

All the same, it was in my mind about the huntsman; an' afther a bit I slipped along by the sallies to see how Mr Anthony was gettin' on.

I could hear the spade goin' as if it was half a dozen men digging: an' troth, afther a minit, I couldn't persuade myself that there wasn't more than wan at it.

'Lord,' sez I, afther listenin' again, 'am I bewitched?' For, sure enough, there was another spade goin' on the far side av the sallies from Mr Anthony.

I keeked through the bushes, an' who was diggin' away for dear life but Ruddell the huntsman himself!

I looked at him, an' looked at him, an' then I rubbed my eyes an' looked at him again; and it was still Ruddell. The first thought in my mind was to warn Mr Anthony, an' I into the wee thicket an' makes for him. But I was too dumbfoundhered to mind my feet, an', before I was well started, I tripped over a rush-bush an' down like a bullock.

'I've done it,' sez I, an' I had.

The huntsman quit diggin' at once, looked round him, and slipped quietly over to the bushes, spade in hand, an' the same minit I hears Mr Anthony stop dead.

'Begad,' sez I to myself, 'it's all up wi' Mr Anthony now.' An' the next minit he riz up face to face with the huntsman across a sally-bush.

Ye never seen two men so much taken aback in your life. They just stood there with their mouths openin' and shuttin' like the goldfish in a bowl.

But Mr Anthony was the worst stuck av the two; for the spade fell from his hand, an' it was the huntsman spoke first.

'Mr Anthony, sir,' sez he, touchin' his hat, 'ye'll not say anythin'.'

It wasn't just what I was expectin', I may tell ye, or Mr Anthony either. But he hadn't served his time in the law courts for nothin'.

'Certainly not, huntsman,' sez he. 'I'll not breathe a word av it.' Ye'd ha' thought by the tone av him he was doin' the man a favour, an' all the time his knees knockin' together, as I knowed right well.

'The fact is, Mr Anthony, sir,' sez the huntsman, 'wan av my hounds strayed to-day, an' I doubt,' sez he, lowerin' his voice till I could hardly hear him, 'I doubt he has been huntin' game an' one av Miss Armytage's keepers has come on him, for I found him here in the bushes with a charge in him. I'm just goin' to bury him quietly here, an' say nothin' about it. You'll say nothin' either, sir, if ye please.'

'Well,' sez I to myself, 'if Mr Anthony ever tells me he's unlucky afther this!'

But it wouldn't be him if he'd let his luck alone.

'You can depend on me, huntsman,' sez he — an' ye could hear the delight av him in his voice — 'ye can depend on me. We'll shake hands on it, huntsman,' sez he, 'we'll shake hands on it!'

The huntsman looked at him in a wondherin' kind av a way.

'Certainly, Mr Anthony, sir,' sez he. An' he reached out his hand.

An' as he leaned across the bush his eye fell first on the grave an' then on the spade at Mr Anthony's feet.

The whole thing flashed on him in a twinklin'.

'I might ha' knowed who it was shot my dog, Mr Anthony,' sez he, very low an' bitther. 'When I seen you with a gun in your hands this afthernoon I might ha' knowed that the pack wasn't safe in the same county with ye, let alone the same town-land. Ye're a danger to every man that walks the road, an' to every man's baste. But this'll be an end to your shootin' — an' to your huntin' too. I've put up with a good deal from ye, Mr Anthony, an' said nothin'. Ye thramped two good pups lame on me the first ye were on a horse this season; the off fore-leg av my best mount'll never grow hair again where that ould grey screw av yours kicked him last November; an' the same dirty brute beat in two panels av the stag-cart on St Stephen's Day, an' all the time I never raised my voice.

'But this is too much. To go an' shoot the best hound in the pack, an' then bury him an' never say ye did it or were sorry for it. It's more than any man could thole. Forbye that ye stood there an' listened to me makin' a fool av meself an' blamin' the poor innocent brute wi' chasin' the game. I take that worst av all. A gentleman wouldn't do it, an' I'll have the opinion av the Hunt on that. I will. I'll –.'

An' on he went like a mill-race. I didn't think the huntsman had it in him.

All the time Mr Anthony just stood there.

'Why the divil,' sez I to meself, 'does he not offer the man a five pound note to keep it dark! Sure it's worth ten times that to him to save the exposin' he'll get.' I could hardly sit quiet for wantin' to get at his ear.

An' wi' that Mr Anthony turns round to the road an' lets out a shout: 'Pat — Pat Murphy!'

Ye could ha' knocked me down with a feather.

'Oh, the weary take ye for a blundherin' wee dundherhead,' sez I to meself, 'are ye not content wi' makin' a byword av yourself but ye must bring me into it. An' me a tenant av Miss Armytage's too. I'm ruined, ruined an' desthroyed. She may put you off the shootin', but she'll dhrive me out av the counthry.'

For a minit, I swithered would I show myself. But, thinks I, he has sold me now, an' I may as well face the music.

So I doubles back along the sallies, an' then comes runnin' up, by the way I was just straight from the road. An' all the prayers Mr Anthony had prayed on himself that day, an' that wasn't a few, was nothin' to what I called down on his head in the time it took me to cover twenty-five yards av ground.

'Have ye done now, huntsman?' sez Mr Anthony as I come up.

'No, nor half done,' sez the huntsman, still ragin' away. An' troth, by the sound av him, he could have kept on for a fortnight, an' never repeated himself.

'Well, give me my turn,' sez Mr Anthony. 'Pick up that spade, Pat.' An' away he walks to where the gander was lyin', an' picks it up.

'Well, by all the saints,' sez I to meself, 'are ye not even goin' to make a fight for it?'

'Do ye see that, huntsman?' sez Mr Anthony, comin' back. 'Wait a minit, now,' sez he, holdin' up his hand, 'an' then ye can talk for a week. Do ye know what that is? It's one av Miss Armytage's prize geese. There's the ring about its leg. When I looked back as I was walkin' along the road wi' Pat Murphy, an hour ago, I saw your dog wi' that goose by the neck an' the goose was dead. Isn't that so, Pat?'

'It's the gospel truth, huntsman,' sez I.

Ye could see the huntsman's jaw dhroppin'.

'Now, Ruddell,' sez Mr Anthony, 'ye were a man I had some respect for till ten minutes ago. An' once or twice when my horse has been a bit restive' — I turned away my head — 'ye have been civiller than many another man in your position would have been. An' I know what happens to a pack av hounds that would kill anybody's geese, let alone Miss Armytage's; an' I shot your dog an' was goin' to bury him here, an' the goose too, an' say nothin' about it. I'll say nothin' about it yet,' sez Mr Anthony, 'an neither will Pat, here. But if your pack av mangy mongrels was to eat every bird an' beast in Miss Armytage's demesne, an' finish up wi' the two stuffed peacocks in the entrance hall, they may do it for me from this day on. Bury your confounded dog,' sez Mr Anthony, by the way av bein' in a rage — an' troth, by this time I think he was beginnin' to believe in himself — 'an' go into mournin' for him if ye like; it's nothin' to me —.'

'Mr Anthony, sir,' sez the huntsman, breakin' in — an' ye never seen a man as much come down in your life — 'I haven't a word to say.'

'It's a change,' sez Mr Anthony.

'Well, I was vexed, sir,' sez the huntsman. 'But I should have knowed betther. Will ye look over what I said? I'm a bit hasty, I know, an' ye'll admit the thing looked queer. But it was kindly done av ye, Mr Anthony, an' it's not every man would ha' had the wit to think av it.

'Ye've saved the credit av the pack, an' me, too; an' I'll not forget it to ye. An' if ye'll excuse me for the impidence I give ye, an'll come out again to the hunt, ye may thramp every hound in the pack, and kick the stag-box into pipe-lights, before I'll say black is the colour av your eye.

'Ye offered to shake hands wi' me, a minit ago. Will ye shake hands now, sir, an' let bygones be bygones?'

'Not a word now, huntsman,' sez Mr Anthony grippin' him by the hand. 'An' there's somethin' to make up the loss av the dog. Now say no more. There, Pat, bury that gander. An' do you cover up the dog, huntsman. The sooner we're out av this the better. Good-bye, huntsman. You can depend on me — an' Pat, too.'

'Good-bye, sir,' sez the huntsman. 'Ye're a gentleman, Mr Anthony, every inch av ye.'

When I caught up wi' Mr Anthony he was in great feather.

'I bamboozled him, Pat, eh?' sez he, chucklin' to himself. 'I bamboozled him, what? The great thing in a case av this sort is to take the right line av defence; an' I saw it in a minit. Damme,' sez Mr Anthony, 'but I'm thrown away as a solicitor, I should have been at the bar.'

'Ye should be in the dock,' sez I; 'an' will be yet if ye don't throw that gun behind the fire.'

'Get away, ye old croaker,' sez Mr Anthony. 'Could ye have bowled over that gander any better than I did? I'll be blest,' sez he, 'if I don't get ould Brown fo fix the lock, an' come back an' have a slap at the wild geese the first clear night. There would nobody see us, Pat.'

'There'll nobody see me,' sez I; 'for I won't be there.'

'Now, ye'll come with me, Pat,' sez Mr Anthony, stoppin' at the foot av the loanin'. 'We can't get into a worse hole than we did today; an' ye saw the way I got us out av it.'

'Well, get the lock fixed first av all, Mr Anthony,' sez I, 'an' then we can talk it over. There'll be a full moon in a week or so.'

'You're right, Pat,' sez he, 'you're right. I'll go up to ould Brown in the mornin'. The full moon, then, Pat. It's a bargain. Good night. I'll be up with Brown before my breakfast tomorrow.'

An' away he goes, hot-foot, as if he thought the moon might come to the full before he got home.

'Don't forget — the full moon,' he calls out as he turned the corner.

'All right, Mr Anthony,' I shouted back. 'The full moon.'

But the next time Mr Anthony an' me goes out shootin' wild geese together there'll be two moons in the sky — an' one in the garden.

Sense and Sawdust

Mr Anthony, the solicitor, said Mr Murphy, was one av them people that think they can do any other body's job better nor their own. I'd watched him makin' a holy show av himself at a deal av things in my time, an' often said he would end up in a circus. Bad an' all as he was, though, I never thought my words would come true. But if a man has a bee in his bonnet there's no tellin' how it'll bizz; an' this is what happened to him in the end.

As long as I mind there was only wan circus came round our part av the world, Simons' Circus. A sore trial it used to be to some av the small fry av us at school; for ould Mackenzie the schoolmaster used to take a special delight in dictating them two words to the wee fellows in the third class, an' then lambastin' everyone that had been trapped into spellin' Circus with an *S*.

Ould Simons died, but the circus still continued in his name, an' passed from one to the other till it fell into the hands av one Hennessey, a big red-faced, bull-necked man with a wicked bad temper. He used to work the most av it off on the horses an' wild animals; an' wan time when the circus came to Ballygullion for the Fair week Miss Armytage av The Hall sent for the ould Cruelty to Animals an' had Hennessey summoned to the Petty Sessions for ill-treatin' a tiger.Hennessey was advised to employ Mr Anthony, an' it was good advice as it turned out, for Mr Anthony, that was never wantin' in some sort av fool cleverness, incited Hennessey to drug the tiger an' then fetch the magistrates down to show them what good friends him an' it was. But the lion-tamer spent the money he got for laudanum for the tiger on whiskey for himself, an' when Hennessey came up to the bars the tiger near tore the ear off him; an' the magistrates unanimously said the brute deserved all it got, an' dismissed the case against Hennessey.

But if the tiger got its claws into Hennessey it was nothin' to the way

Hennessey got his claws in Mr Anthony. From the day Hennessey first consulted him the pair av them was brothers. In the mornin' you'd see Mr Anthony headin' up to the circus with a pair av ridin' breeches on him that made him look as if the Almighty had give him a deal more provision for sittin' down than for standin' up; an' in the afthernoon you'd see him going' back again in a gymnasium costume to learn tumblin'. He wasn't fit to speak to at all, for the divil a thing he could talk about but trick-ridin' an' conjurin'. An' when the circus left Ballygullion, an' he could only get in touch with it every weekend, his chief clerk told me he spent most av his time in the office practisin' high kickin' an' readin' Barnum's life av himself.

Then all at once there came a change; an' like most av the changes that come on Mr Anthony it was a clean roundabout wan. You had only to mention a circus to him to start him swearin' like a bona-fide traveller in a Temperance Hotel; an' the day he called Hennessey nothin' worse than a cats'-meat man he was in a by-ordinary good temper.

'What's gone wrong with you, Mr Anthony?' sez I to him wan day, at the last. 'It's no time since you were clean mad on circuses, an' goin' to put money in wan if you got the chance. What change has come over you at all?'

It was in his own office I was speakin' to him, an' he just riz up an' kicked a big law-book into single leaves.

'I *have* put money in a circus,' sez he, 'a hundred an' fifty good-lookin' pounds that I lent that pig-faced whiskey-vault, Hennessey; an' it'll never come out again. The circus is insolvent. It's only three weeks since I lent Hennessey the last fifty, an' the very next day I had to threaten a writ on him for a client av mine. Not that I mind the money,' sez he. 'What about it. It's the stupidity an' jealousy av the man I object to. There was I, just to his hand. Before I'd had two days' trainin' he must have seen I was the makin's av one av the finest all-round performers in the history av the ring. But would he make use av me? — I offered, with two or three weeks' more trainin', to take the leadin' part in the programme an' set the concern on its legs within six months; an', damme, the big bloated human porter-bottle just laughed at me.'

'Oh, well, Mr Anthony,' sez I, humorin' him, 'a gentleman like you has no call about a circus.'

'Now that's where you're wrong, Pat,' sez he. 'A man av brains will come to the front anywhere. There were things about a circus that I could have done. Trick horsemanship wasn't one av them, I'll admit. I'm too much av the plain hard-riding cross-countryman for that. But there were other things I could have done. You should just have seen, for example, the shape I made at jugglin'. Will you believe it, but before the end av the Fair week I could keep Snell's *Equity*, an' Robinson's *Wills,* an' Mackenzie's *Conveyancing* all in the air at the wan time. If I hadn't kicked the cover av Snell a minit ago I'd show you now. But do you know what I'd really have made, Pat?' sez he. He lowered his voice an' looked round the office before he spoke. '*A clown*,' sez he.

'Aw, blethers, Mr Anthony,' sez I. 'Who put that in your head. Hennessey, I suppose?'

'Not a bit av him,' sez Mr Anthony. 'He hasn't the gumption. Do you mind havin' a drink with me an' wan av the circus people in Fair week — a dark little man about my size? That was Hennessey's clown. A fine little fellow, that. No professional jealousy about him at all. He told me if I'd been trained to his job from a child I'd have been the greatest clown since Grimaldi. I've all the gifts, he said. I can dance, as you know, Pat; an' I'm more than a bit av a gymnast. It was only yesterday I kicked the barometer off the wall there, an' it five feet from the ground. An' as for a comic fall — well, I fell on my belly for him in Michael Cassidy's shug that night, an' he near died.'

'Ay,' sez I, 'an' you fell one day when you were out with me with a gun in your hand, an' I was a d——d sight nearer dyin'. Clown!' sez I. 'Will you have a bit av sense, an' go on collectin' six-an'-eightpences, or you'll wake up some fine mornin' an' find yourself doing clown in a padded cell.'

'Is it six-an'-eightpences!' sez Mr Anthony, sweepin' two sticks av red sealin'-wax into eternity with a wave av his hand. 'Do you hear me, Pat? Saunders — that's Hennessey's clown — says I have a high cackle av a comic laugh that would be worth fifty pounds a week to me in London. Wait a minit till you hear,' sez he, openin' the door into the public office softly. 'No, there's someone there. But, curse it,' sez he, throwin' himself down in his chair, 'if Hennessey had as much brains as a tenpenny nail could pick out av a whelk, we'd both have made our fortunes. He'll be sorry yet. I get my law cheap, an' if I don't put that big livin' blancmange into the Bankruptcy Court my name's not Anthony.'

About three weeks afther our talk I got a letter from him to call in. When I entered the private office he began to dance a jig.

'I've done it, Pat,' sez he, 'I've done it. Didn't I tell you I'd do it. Stand back till you see me throwin' a cart-wheel!' He made a kind av an awkward spang on the floor, an' as he came right side up he near knocked a piece out av the steel safe with his head.

'Are you killed, Mr Anthony?' sez I, runnin' over to him.

'I'm all right,' sez he, staggerin' round the room like a new-dhropped calf, an' gropin' for the eyeglass with the hand he wasn't rubbin' his head with. 'It's the man that designed this hat-box av a room that should be killed. Never mind, it'll not be long till I have room to do more than that. Did you hear the news, Pat? Hennessey's busted, an' the circus is bein' wound up.'

'Oh, my father, Mr Anthony,' sez I, 'don't tell me you've bought the circus!'

'Ah,' sez Mr Anthony, skippin' round in great delight, 'I know you would think that, you brainless old omadhaun. You'll never learn sense, not even by associatin' with me. No, I didn't buy the circus. Did you ever know me do a foolish thing yet? But I'll tell you what I did. I got myself appointed receiver, an' the whole thing is to be handed over to me — tents, caravans, dresses, horses, lions, tiger an' all. Where's the inventory?' sez he, divin' into a heap av papers as if he was going off a spring-board. 'Never mind, it's somewhere. But there's enough property to pay thirty shillings in the pound, an' even if there isn't I can easy knock my own hundred an' fifty out av the windin'-up expenses. *Buy* the circus,' sez he, curlin' up his lip at me, 'why, man, I'm gettin' money for takin' it for nothing!'

'I suppose you'll sell out everything at once?' sez I.

'Sell,' sez he, 'sell?' The bulge in his eyes near knocked his eye-glass off. 'An' me with a whole circus to myself. Damme, you're mad. Listen, Pat,' sez he, 'this is the first real chance I've ever had in my life av showin' what an organizer has been buried among a heap av old sheepskins. I'm goin' to show first Ballygullion, an' then all Ireland the spectacle av the only circus that has ever been run intelligently since Noah exercised the animals afther the Flood. As for any little performance that I may throw in from time to time if receipts are sinkin' at all, I suppose I'll have to do them in disguise. But don't you think, Pat,' sez he, lookin' at me a bit anxious, 'that even if I did paint my face, something about me would be sure to leak out?'

'You'll be famous from Rathlin Island to the Cove av Cork, Mr Anthony,' sez I. 'That is, if you're not devoured by one av the lions — or by Hennessey.'

An' away I goes down the street, laughin', for I couldn't persuade myself that he'd meant half he'd been sayin'.

But he had. An' as long as he confined himself to the business side av things he didn't do too badly. For, mind ye, although they were all juggled up with a whole lot av mad-headedness, Mr Anthony had brains.

First av all he hired a big field near Ballygullion an' assembled the whole show there, horses, an' carriages, an' tents, an' caravans, an' human bein's, an' what people call dumb animals, though God knows they nearly roared the place down. The whole rickmatick av them was no sooner there than trainin' began for the next tour. Hennessey done the gafferin' under Mr. Anthony's direction, an' before a fortnight had lost about two stone weight, an' got a scunner at Mr Anthony that near give him the jaundice.

However, if Mr Anthony had made an enemy he balanced it with a friend, for he'd seen that the little clown fellow was real smart an' brought his part av the performance a lot more to the front. There's no doubt it made the whole entertainment more light-hearted an' takin' altogether. An' as for Saunders, the clown, he'd have let Mr Anthony clean his boots on him.

The day drew near for the circus to set out. Mr Anthony by this time had bamboozled the creditors into acceptin' seven-an'-sixpence in the pound, an' he calculated that he could clear that in wan tour. His own debt was to be paid in full if he earned the seven-an'-sixpence for the creditors, an' he was to get a thumpin' good fee as well. I begun to think he'd maybe stick to common sense an' business, seein' how well it was goin' to pay him. Besides, he had got wan or two setbacks in his notions about performin'. The cleverness av little Saunders had daunted him a good deal in the matter av doin' clown; an' afther loosenin' his whole front teeth on the edge av a zinc bucket tryin' to throw a back somersault, he decided to take up somethin' not so active. So he got in tow with the Contortionist an' Handcuff King, an' had some lessons from him. But, first av all, he tangled himself up so badly in his own office chair that they had to get in Sam Robins, the carpenter, to cut him out with a saw so as he'd be in time for the Petty Sessions. Then wan Sunday mornin' he invited a polis constable into his private house to put a pair av handcuffs on him an' said he'd get himself out av them in ten minutes. At the end av two hours when they sent down to the barracks for the key the sergeant wouldn't give it up owin' to him havin' been very badly worsted by Mr Anthony in a licensin' case the day before. So they sent for the Handcuff King; but though he may have been King av his own handcuffs, he wasn't even Prince av Wales av the polis ones. All he liberated was about a quart av Mr Anthony's whiskey out av a jar, an' it wasn't till the sergeant had to come up in the afthernoon to arrest him for tryin' to set fire to himself that Mr Anthony was released. By that time he was purty well cured av both contortions an' handcuffs, I may tell you; so the circus started out on tour without him, an' he said it might go to hell.

But when it was gone he was like a child with a broken toy, all heavy an' discontented, an' not a word out av him. Great reports came in about the money it was liftin' an' that made him all the worse; because he had hoped they couldn't do without him. The only time I saw him perkin' up was when a travellin' fellow came to Ballygullion one market-day an' untied himself out av a knotted rope. Mr Anthony was greatly interested an' said the travellin' man knowed a deal more nor the Handcuff King. And so he did, too, for he went round to Mr Anthony's that evening to give him the tip av it all, an' tied him up in his own garden an' took five pound ten out av his pocket when he couldn't move, and run off an' was never heard av again.

Reports av the circus still kept on good, an' great mention was bein' made av wee Saunders, the clown. Mr Anthony stood it for a while longer, but at last he could thole no more, an' off he went. He didn't appear again for over a week an' when he did he sent for me as usual. I wasn't right in till he was on his feet with the eyes dancin' in his head.

'Pat,' sez he, 'I'm a fool. Saunders was right. It's a clown I should be. The clown's *the* thing in a circus. Of course I saw that when I took the circus over. But I gave Saunders his chance. It's the poor fellow's bread an' butter, an' I wanted him to make his reputation before I butted in. He's good, mind you; damme, he's good. But when I appear he'll just fade away. He painted me up the other night an' let me go on an' pick up the properties; an', blast me, but the very stable helpers were splittin' their sides at me. I did a comic fall over a tetherin'-rope that fair made people scream, an' if I'd seen the rope in time I could have done it twice as well. Goodbye, now,' sez he fussin' into his chair an' takin' up a pen, 'I must get to work. The circus'll be back here in two months, an' I've got to have the whole tricks av the trade at my fingers' ends before then.'

'But why by that time, Mr Anthony?' sez I, though I knew in my heart what was comin'.

'Pat,' sez Mr Anthony, forgettin' all about his work; an' leppin' to his feet again, 'in two months' time the people av Ballygullion are goin' to have the treat av their lives. Saunders has agreed to make me up like him, an' I'm to do clown here for the first night, an' if all goes well, maybe for the second too. What do you think av that, eh?'

He took a skip or two an' gave his eyeglass a couple av whirls on the end av the string that sent the bits av it hoppin' off the desk like hailstones.

'But Hennessey,' sez I, when I'd got my breath. 'What'll Hennessey say?'

'Hennessey to a hot place,' sez Mr Anthony, snappin' his fingers. 'I won't ask his leave. Between you an' me I've found him out cookin' the accounts, an' if he says a word I'll let him know it. So there we are. You'll come to see me the night I'm on?'

'If I'm alive I'll be there,' sez I. 'An' if I'm dead I'll come back an' haunt the circus for the night.'

An' I meant it. If I'd died before that performance there wasn't a tombstone in Ireland would have held me down.

I went round to Mr Anthony's house in three or four weeks' time, an', 'deed, I'll admit he was makin' a wonderful attempt. Provided he didn't break his neck before the big night, he was goin' to pass as far as the tumblin' business was concerned, an' he had hit on a notion av wearin' a wee moustache on his nose that, if it looked as funny on a clown as it did on a solicitor, was goin' to make history, in Ballygullion at any rate.

When at long last the circus did come back the wee clown admitted as much.

'I don't mind telling you, Mr Murphy,' sez he to me in Cassidy's pub, 'the little gentleman is a fair knock-out for brains. Why,' sez he, 'I got tips off him myself. I can't say more than that. That nose moustache av his is fair genius. 'Enery Irving in his day never thought av better. And as for his falls, well, he don't mean 'em, leastways not the way they come off, but every wan av 'em's a round in itself. Don't you be uneasy about him. Mind your mind easy, either, Mr Murphy. I'll watch over 'im like a mother. 'E's a little duke, 'e is. An' short av 'is bustin' 'is little boiler on a tent-peg 'e can't come to any great 'arm.'

As I went home from Cassidy's that evenin' I felt for the first time that the whole fool business might come off, afther all. An' when I begun to think av it I couldn't see what harm, short av Mr Anthony being' struck off the rolls. Of course everybody about the circus in the know was swore to hold his tongue, but afther the first performance it was all sure to come out. However, the whole world knew what Mr Anthony was by this time, an' would give him a fool's pardon. I went to my bed that night with my mind purty well at ease, an' next night — the big night, that was — I declare I ran the last quarter av a mile to the circus like a wee boy av ten.

The clown an' I were to sit together in the shilling seats, the clown with a false beard on to hide himself from the public. Mr Anthony wouldn't let him stay behind, for, as he said, cute enough, if he got cold feet, an' the real clown was available, he mightn't face the music at the last minit.

When I got to the entrance where I was to meet wee Saunders, he was waitin' for me.

'Sorry, Mr Murphy,' sez he, 'but I'm afraid I'll have to go on afther all.'

I was half sorry too, but more pleased.

'I never thought he'd do it when it came to the bit,' sez I.

'No, no,' sez Saunders, 'it's not *'im*. 'E's game all right. But 'Ennessey's kicked. Won't let 'im go on. Says it's not professional. Blimey,' sez Saunders, 'a man that would pick pockets, an' 'e won't take good money because a thing's not professional. Twenty good quid it was worth to me, an' wasn't it me was riskin' my reputation, not 'im. But 'alf a mo, till I go round to the dressing tent again. The little gentleman 'as got the 'alf-Nelson on 'im over some dirty work about money, an' maybe 'e'll manage 'im yet.'

Presently back comes Saunders, rubbin' his hands.

'It's all right,' sez he, ''Ennessey's caved. The little gentleman fair put it up to him. Jail or the show; that was what 'e said. But, by gum, 'Ennessey's not 'alf in a rage. Lord help the horses tonight. But come along, Mr Murphy. This 'ere'll be worth seein'.'

The circus was well filled an' everybody seemed pleased with the performance, but as for me I couldn't take anythin' in at all, I was that excited. I don't know how long it was before there was any word av Mr Anthony, but I felt as if it was about a week. At last wee Saunders grips me by the arm.

'Look out!' sez he, ''e's comin' now. Watch this. 'E's to stand on a loose rope, the way he did once by accident, an' do a fall as the horse pulls it tight. If this comes off 'is whole show'll start with a bang.'

The words weren't out av his mouth till in comes Mr Anthony painted up till his own mother would have set the dog on him. There was a great roar av applause.

'Of course they think it's me,' sez Saunders in my ear.

Mr Anthony bowed, an' then run forward very cautious, looking for the rope. I could swear he'd have give a pound for his eyeglass. Just as he got within four or five feet av the rope he slipped. Down he went on his face, the horse was whipped on, an' up riz the rope. It took Mr Anthony somewhere about the neck an' turned him in a back somersault that just planted his heels fair in the pit av Hennessey's stomach as he followed Mr Anthony in his tall hat an' big whip. Mr Anthony riz up, an' Hennessey was helped up, an' stood there a minit or two hardly able to move. But there was no hurry. The people was fair laughin' themselves sick, an' as for wee Saunders I thought he was goin' into hysterics. Presently Hennessey followed Mr Anthony into the ring, an' whether it was rage or the dunt he'd got in his dinner, I can't tell, but he was green in the face.

However, nobody looked at him. Between the way he had made his entrance an' the comic appearance av him with the wee moustache on his nose, Mr Anthony had the whole house in stitches. Whatever he did was funny. The things he meant to do was funny, an' the things he done that he didn't mean to do was fit to burst your sides. He tripped an' he fell, backwards an' forwards an' sideways an' undher horses' feet; an' horses fell over him, an' wan av the performing dogs that he stood on by mistake bit him in the leg av his costume an' near choked itself on wan av the wee black balls av wool that was sewed on it. An' if things was fallin' a bit flat at all Mr Anthony had only to twirl the ends av the moustache on his nose an' give wan av his unearthly cackles av a laugh, an' the whole house would screech. As for me, I was just a wee boy again an' laughed at anythin' or nothin' as I'd never thought to laugh again.

And then all at once there was a change. We came to the part near the end where the clown an' the ring-master begin to sauce each other, an' then falls out. Hennessey pretends to get angrier an' angrier — an', 'deed, I thought he was actin' it uncommon well — an' then he by the way av takes the whip to the clown.

The first slash, I seen Mr Anthony lepp very like as if he was hurted; an' I jumped myself.

'It's all right,' whispers Saunders, ''E's well padded where 'e's bein' hit. What's that?' sez he, drawin' his breath sharp as there came another lash. 'Stay there, Mr Murphy,' he calls in my ear through the noise av the laughin', ''Ennessey's gone barmy!' An' off he tears, but I seen it would take him ages to push his way out.

I sat there, holdin' on to the seat to keep myself from shoutin'. For there was no doubt about it. Hennessey wasn't hittin' the padded places at all, an' was fair torturing Mr Anthony. The squirms an' lepps av the poor wee man was something by-ordinary. The crowd simply yelled with delight as the spangs av him got more outrageous, an' though I was ready to cry with vexation an' rage there was times I had to laugh in spite av myself. An' all the time Mr Anthony, with the entrance gapin' wide for him, kept in the ring an' carried on his part. An' when the end came, an' the quarrel was supposed to be made up, an' he kneeled down to ask pardon, he smiled up in Hennessey's face as if he liked him. I'll say this for Mr Anthony, if he hasn't a deal av sense he has a great heart, anyway.

I had to stand a long while outside waitin' for him, an' when he did come out with Saunders at his heels, he beckoned me away round to the back av the big tent. I could hardly wait till we got there.

'How are you, Mr Anthony?' sez I. 'Are you all right? Was he hittin' you in earnest?'

'Earnest!' sez Mr Anthony. 'If there was such a thing as a red an' white wan, nothin' but the polis would prevent me appearin' tomorrow night as a zebra. I'm half raw, Pat,' sez he, 'but, damme, it was worth it. Did you notice the activity av me, twistin' round undher that horse's belly before he knew I'd been on his back? Did you see the lepps av me — like a flea at a Spring cleaning? Without the whip I'd never have done it. I was learnin' the trade with every fresh welt. Have you ever met my equal; now tell me the truth? An' it was nothin' to what I'll be tomorrow night.'

'I never knew anything like you, Mr Anthony,' sez I, shakin' him by the hand, 'an' never will again. But I'll not be there tomorrow night to see you maybe mistreated again by that big ruffian.'

'You will be there,' sez Mr Anthony, 'an' if you don't see that big jelly-fish-faced Guy Fawkes bitin' the dust I'll never draft another lease. Listen to me, Pat. One more good house there must be, an' then the composition is paid, an' I'm paid. An' by the time I'm finished with Hennessey he can have what's left, an' welcome. I'm not a vindictive man,' sez he, 'but when I have reason to believe I'm ill-treated, damme, I see red. Come on, Saunders.' An' away he stalks.

'Mr Murphy,' sez Saunders as he turned to go afther him, 'don't you miss tomorrow night at no price. Only take my tip,' sez he, in a half-whisper, turnin' back, 'sit near the way out.'

By this time nothin' on earth would have made me miss it, whatever it was; an' so long as Hennessey got a downfall I didn't care very much.

Next evenin' when I went into Ballygullion here wasn't the whole town plastered with Hennessey's bills sayin' that the new clown at Simons' Circus would give positively his last appearance — at double prices. Before I was in the town ten minutes I found everybody knew the clown was Mr Anthony. Such a scene as the circus field was you never saw in your day. I met people there that I knew had come five miles, however the news reached them. Four polismen could hardly keep the crowd from makin' matches av the pay-box, an' I heard aftherwards that the cashier got rid av all the bad money, in change, that the circus had been stuck with for the previous five years. Some people was vexed about the double prices, but most av them paid up like men an' said it was well worth the money, only to see Mr Anthony.

By the time I got in, the place was more like the inside av a tin av sardines than a circus, an' if I could have been sure that the middle pole av the tent would fall on some bigger sinner than me I'd have been happier in my mind. As for the programme, it didn't matter very much. All any av us wanted to see was Mr Anthony. An', troth, he was good, better in some ways than the night before, though worse in others. His fallin' about wasn't just as outrageous, but I wasn't surprised, with the state his back must have been in. But he had been working up the business av the comic moustache till he could make it squirm on his nose like a live thing, an' the people laughed themselves silly at him.

What puzzled me at first was Hennessey not bein' there, for there was another man doin' his part. Then I twigged, av course, that Mr Anthony was takin' no risks about the whip. But still I was puzzled. I couldn't see how he was to get at Hennessey if Hennessey was away; an' as time wore on an' he didn't appear, I thought nothin' by-ordinary was goin' to happen at all.

The performance ended as usual with the clown kneeling down before the ring-master, an' the ring-master bestowin' a bunch av carrots on him. Then the people riz to their feet an' I thought the tent would have split with the yells an' the calls av 'Mr Anthony, Mr Anthony'. And then, just as I was goin' to turn away, very much disappointed, I may tell you, out comes Hennessey himself with a big silver cup an' holds up his hand for silence when he did.

'Ladies an' gentlemen,' sez he, 'in order to acknowledge the debt I am under to him an' to show the good feeling that has always existed between the two av us, I wish to present this cup to my good friend —' here the clown was pushed forward — 'my good friend Mr Anthony —'

He got no further. All at once there was a hiss like everybody in the circus drawing their breath at the one time, an' here, across the ring, towards the way out, walks Mr Anthony himself in his overcoat an' hat, lookin' as unlike a clown as anythin' you ever seen in your life. I looked at the real clown an' *he* was makin' for the way out as well. An' then I saw it all, an' in about two seconds more the crowd saw it too.

Up till then Hennessey had been starin' afther Mr Anthony in a dazed kind av a way, but when the crowd rushed at him he woke up to realities an' took to his heels. It was nothin' short av a miracle that he wasn't massacred. As I heard the story aftherwards, two or three av the leaders would get their hands on him every now an' then an' pull somethin' more off him, an' then he'd fight himself clear till he'd be caught again. But they all got round him at the gate av the circus field, an' there's no doubt he'd have been killed there if Mrs Moloney's goat hadn't got into the middle av the crowd an' been taken for the tiger. Every man ran for his life, but Hennessey beat them all an' got clean away. By the time people found their wits again an' went back to wreck the circus, enough av the polis had gathered to save a good deal av it.

When most av the stir was over I walked round to Mr Anthony's house an' found him tryin' an old false moustache on his nose.

'Well, you ought to go to bed satisfied to-night, Mr Anthony,' sez I. 'You've cleared the circus av debt, an' you've paid friend Hennessey out for his whippin', an' now you're free av all this clown business. For, afther what has happened, if you went down on your bended knees nobody will believe you appeared last night either.'

Mr Anthony turned round from the glass, an' if he had minded to take the moustache off his nose he'd have been very serious-lookin'.

'Do you know, Pat,' sez he, 'that's just what's stickin' in my gizzard. Saunders thought av this business to-night, not me. He planned it all an' played on the quarrel I had with Hennessey to get me to consent to it. I begin to see why, now that it's too late. He was just jealous, Pat, professional jealousy. He wanted me out av the way, that's all. I can never go back to the ring now, an' I'll lose millions by it. You saw the crowd was there to-night when they only thought it was me, but think av the multitudes would be there tomorrow if it *had* been me!'

He was quite serious, too; an', troth, as I went down the road home it come intil my head that there was many a sensibler man than Mr Anthony in an asylum, let alone doin' clown.

A Sweepstake

The whole trouble started with Mr Barrington av the Bank givin' a card party the night wee Mr Anthony, the solicitor, was dinin' with the district inspector av the polis.

Mr Anthony an' Mr Barrington were both reasonably young bachelors at the time, an' both went to lodge with a Mrs Shanks, a respectable widow with a thirsty son. Mr Anthony had the dinin'-room upstairs; but the pair av them bein' good friends they clubbed rooms, an' ate together in the dinin'-room an' sat together in the sittin'-room. To save trouble an' expense they shared the same meals, an' went halves in the cost. But a man's eatin' depends on himself, an' his drinkin' depends on his friends; an' they thought it better for each man to have his own whiskey-bottle.

The night av Mr Barrington's party Jim Cochrane, the vet, was in bad luck; but, as Mr Barrington said aftherwards, if he lost on the cards he won on the whiskey; for to drown his sorrows he drank as much as the other four put together, with the result that Mr Barrington's bottle ran dry.

This was awkward; for though it was far too soon to give up their game, it was afther ten o'clock, the closin' hour for the pubs in them days. A kind av a depression fell on the party as they eyed the empty bottle; an' Mr Barrington began to feel very small, although he couldn't fairly be blamed for Jim Cochrane's drouth.

All at once he had a great idea.

'Boys,' he sez, 'Mr Anthony has half a bottle in the sideboard. We'll drink that, an' I'll restore it to him tomorrow. He'll want no drink, comin' from the D.I.'s house, I know.'

Mr Anthony's half-bottle went the way av the rest, and about twelve o'clock they were playin' the last hand before they'd go home, when they heard the hall-door open.

'That'll be Anthony,' sez Mr Barrington. 'Play your card, Jim.'

But Jim Cochrane held his hand, an' still listened; an' a kind av an uneasy silence fell on the crowd. The next thing they heard was Mr Anthony's voice:

'Come in, Tom, an' have a deoch-an-doris. I can give you a dhrop av the best whiskey in Ireland.'

With that Mr Anthony skips into the room, salutes everybody very friendly, an' goes over to the sideboard. He lifted out his bottle, looked at it, an' held it up to the light — Oh divil a squig!

Everybody expected an explosion; but Mr Anthony never said wan syllable, but put the bottle back, closed the sideboard door very carefully, an' walked out av the room. The card-party finished very soon afther, an' though there was an attempt at laughin' at Mr Anthony's misfortune, an' some half-hearted chaff about him takin' the matter to the Courts, the boys went down Mrs Shanks's steps with their tails very much between their legs.

Mr Barrington an' me was sittin' in the private bar av Michael Cassidy's pub when he told me this story; an' when he got so far he stopped an' began to laugh.

'Would you believe me, Pat,' sez he, 'but ever since that evenin' the suspicious wee rascal has been hidin' his whiskey-bottle! — Wait though —' he pulled out his watch — 'an' I'll make him admit it in the presence av a witness.'

As he spoke the words round the door comes Mr Anthony, eyeglass an' all, as cocky as usual.

'Certainly I'm hidin' my whiskey,' sez he, 'an' why wouldn't I, Barrington? Blast it, I'm a solicitor, not a spigot. I hope I'm not wanting in hospitality. None av the Anthonys ever were, so far as I know. On the rare occasions when the best solicitor in Ulster does get his fingers on six-an'-eightpence he doesn't mind spending six shillings av it entertaining his friends; but when the last eightpence av it is taken out av his pocket without his leave he draws the line; damme, he draws the line.'

'I never took your blooming whiskey but once,' sez Mr Barrington leppin' to his feet as red as a turkey-cock.

'You'll pardon me, Barrington,' sez Mr Anthony, very cool an' composed. 'Your honour is not in question; but your memory is bad — I'm a methodical man, as you know. I can tell — damme,' sez he, 'I can tell to the blindin' av a midge's eye at any time how much I've taken out av my bottle —'

'Up to about your fifth glass, that is,' put in Mr Barrington.

'D—n the fifth glass,' sez Mr Anthony, leppin' up very red in his turn, 'I never had five glasses at wan time in my life. Listen, Barrington: on Tuesday fortnight you drank out av my bottle from the upper edge av the label to the top av the word "whiskey". Three days afther that you drank down to the bottom av the *"y"*. And last Wednesday night you and your friends finished half-a-bottle on me. You didn't forget about that, I know — dammit,' sez he, 'nobody short av a dipsomaniac could forget half-a-bottle av whiskey. But the other two drinks went clean out av your mind — so I hid my whiskey. I hid it where you nor no other man'll ever find it,' sez he, swellin' himself out. 'Blast it,' sez he. 'I've hid it that well that there's times I can hardly find it myself.'

'You hid it in the chimney,' sez Mr Barrington, givin' another av the easy-goin' grins, 'on the left-hand size av the breast-work av brick that goes round the inside av the chimney.'

Mr Anthony's jaw fell about a foot, an' he looked very foolish.

'How did you find out?' sez he. 'If your bed was in the same room as mine I'd say I must have been talkin' in my sleep.'

'You came up afther dinner, the other night,' sez Mr Barrington, 'with the smell av whiskey on you very strong, an' soot on the knuckles av your right hand. So I looked an' found the bottle. An' now my bottle is sittin' on the same breastwork,' sez he, 'only on the right-hand side. More than that,' he goes on, 'there's a dose in my bottle that the chemist prepared for me; an' if a certain person finds the bottle, as he's sure to do from the stupid way you go on, Anthony —' (Mr Anthony opened his mouth here, but shut it again on second thoughts) 'he'll get the surprise av his young life. It was the landlady's son that lowered the tide for you, Anthony,' sez he, 'an' not me at all. But I fancy this little mixture av mine'll help *his* memory.'

'You're a stupid fool,' sez Mr Anthony, takin' no notice av the dig; 'an' before all's over you'll find yourself in the dock. Why didn't you consult a solicitor, especially when you could have got wan for nothin'. If this mixture is harmful you may be indicted for manslaughter.'

'Ah, blethers,' sez Mr Barrington. 'It'll give the young fellow a gripe that'll make him think he's taken strychnine, that all —'

'Listen, Barrington,' sez Mr Anthony, very serious. 'Listen to a man that everybody in this town knows doesn't give bad advice. Away an' look afther that bottle av yours.'

But at this point I broke in.

'You'd better away an' look afther your own, Mr Anthony,' sez I. 'Big Billy Lenahan was standin' near the door when Mr Barrington said where your whiskey was hid. I misdoubted at the time that he was closer nor was wholesome; an' I misdoubt it far more now, because I see him rollin' his big carcase up towards your lodgin's at the rate av about ten miles an hour.'

But with all his vanity an' capers, Mr Anthony was always the wee gentleman.

'Run like blazes, Barrington,' sez he. 'If he didn't hear clearly, an' mistakes the side av the chimney, that big rascal is the very man to toast you for about five hundred pounds.'

Away the two av them went, an' me with them; for I wasn't goin' to miss the fun. When we got to the lower end av the street Mrs Shanks's house is in we could see Billy on the top av the steps up to the door talkin' to Mrs Shanks herself. He turned an' looked down the street, but I knew he couldn't have seen us, for he went in afther Mrs Shanks an' closed the door.

'Quick march,' sez Mr Anthony in a very military voice all at once. 'I'm in command here.' An' away the three av us goes, heel an' toe.

But it was a long street, an' uphill all the way; an' we were too late. Mrs Shanks was at the door the minit the knocker struck it, all upset-lookin'.

'Oh, Mr Barrington,' sez she, 'God bless you! — A man's just come in to see you, an' he's took terrible bad in the dinin'-room. — Listen,' sez she. 'Oh, run!'

There come a deep groan an' a crash from the dinin'-room as Mr Barrington fumbled at the door-handle; an' when the three av us rushed in there was Billy Lenahan on the floor, rollin' from side to side, tearin' at his throat, an' groanin' somethin' lamentable to hear.

All the time I was puffin' my way up the sreet I'd been prayin', God forgive me, that Billy would drink from Mr Barrington's bottle; but when I saw him squirmin' there in agony, rascal an' all as he was, I wished my prayer hadn't been answered so pat. As for Mr Barrington he went as white as a sheet.

Mr Anthony was tremblin' like a leaf, himself; all the same he took command.

'Stand back,' sez he, squattin' down. 'I hold a certificate in the St John Ambulance. — This man looks to be poisoned, Barrington,' sez he, very professional.

'Oh, go to hell,' shouts Mr Barrington, pushin' him over on his back, an' dhroppin' on his knees beside Big Billy.

'What's wrong, Lenahan?' sez he. 'Are you ill? How do you feel?'

'The pains,' groans Billy. 'The pains. — I'm on fire inside. Oh, Mr Barrington, give me somethin'!' The whites av his eyes turned up in his head, an' the two arms av him stiffened like ramrods.

'Convulsions,' sez Mr Anthony, puttin' the eyeglass back on his face. 'This looks to me like strychnine.'

'Take his head, you fool,' roars Mr Barrington, near cryin'.

He dashes over to the fireplace, stoops down, an' fetches out a bottle av whiskey.

'That's *your* whiskey, you great big ass,' snaps Mr Anthony. 'Give him mine.'

'My heavens,' sez Mr Barrington, holdin' up the bottle, 'an he's put half av it in him. — Quick, Anthony,' he stutters. He pulls out the other bottle from the fireplace; an' runs over to Billy.

'A glass, Pat,' sez he. 'Oh hurry, man,' sez he, pluckin' the cork out with his teeth an' nearly brainin' Mr Anthony with the back av his head. 'A cup — a spoon — anythin'.'

'Put the bottle to his lips, Mr Barrington,' sez I. 'These mountainy men has insides like a boiler.'

An' sure enough, Billy took a long pull at the whiskey an' never even coughed. He leaned back a minit, drew a deep breath an' then put up his lips again like a pet lamb at a suckin' bottle. I could see a good deal av the sympathy leavin' Mr Anthony's face.

'How are you now?' asks Mr Barrington. He pulled the bottle out av Billy's mouth with a plop, sat back on his haunches, an' put the bottle down on the floor.

'Better,' sez Billy, very low an' gaspin'. He half sat up, an' looked round the room.

'Is that you, Pat,' he whispers. 'How do you come to be here? Oh, Pat, I've drunk some terrible thing.'

All at once he let a screech, snapped his teeth together like a rat-trap an' lashed out with his arms an' legs. Mr Anthony went backwards into the fireplace. As he fell the string av his eyeglass lapped round the neck av a wee china lady on the mantelpiece, an' she followed Mr Anthony, only she didn't stay wholc. As for Mr Barrington, wan av Billy's workin' boots had took him in thc waistcoat, an' by the look in his eye as he went two-double round the room he was feelin' near bad enough to drink his own whiskey.

It was all was left for him, anyway. The second convulsion Billy took, his hand encountered the whiskey bottle on the floor. He fell back; his whole body loosened in a second, teeth an' all; an' when the bottle dhropped from his hand there was no whiskey spilled.

I could stand it no longer, but went over an' took him under the armpits.

'Get up, you big humbug,' sez I between my teeth as I lifted at him. 'There was very little the matter with you.'

Big Billy sprachled up on his feet as I expected, now that the drink was done, an' stood there lurchin' back an' forward; an' if he wasn't sick any longer there was no man could say, in any fair play, that he was sober. Mr Anthony was on his feet, too, lookin' very ill-pleased at his empty bottle; an' Mr Barrington was about half straightened-up, an' lookin', no better pleased, at Billy. But Billy got his oar in first.

'You'll rue this, Mr Barrington,' sez he, puttin' his hands in his pockets an' then takin' them out again to balance himself. 'Oh, I know,' sez he. 'This is all because I didn't meet my wee bill at your bank when it fell due. I have your letter, still. If I didn't attend to it you'd do somethin' that would surprise me, eh?' — I wish you'd seen the horror in Mr Barrington's face. 'But to invite me in to have a drink; an' then first — *uck!* — to poison me, an' next to pour whiskey into me that was worse than poison' — I was lookin' at Mr Anthony's face now, an' it was worth while — 'I wouldn't 've believed it av a manager av the Downshire Bank. — But wait,' sez Billy, gettin' thicker with every word. 'There'll be law over this. If there was a s'licitor here that knew the law about anythin' but a poor man makin' — sup av potheen,' sez he, lookin' very wicked at Mr Anthony, 'I'd employ him. As it is,' sez he, 'I'll — *uck*!' — sez he, that unexpected that his hat fell off — 'go to a s'licitor that *does* know law. — Misser Barrington, you'll've a lerrer from Mr Fitzsimons, B.L. — *B.L.,'* he repeats, glarin' at Mr Anthony — 'in the mornin!'

He stooped down for his hat. As he riz he laid hold av the fancy cloth that was on the mantelpiece; an' all I can say is, the wee china lady was buried among her friends. Then he made his way out av the room, an' next minit I heard the front door tryin' if the house was jerry-built. Neither Mr Barrington nor Mr Anthony said one word. I went over to the window an' looked out.

'Well, thank God,' sez I, 'he's fell down the steps, anyway.'

'That he may never get up again for an oily big fraud!' sez Mr Barrington, very hearty. 'This'll be a dear dosin' for me if he can make it.'

But there was more bounce in Mr Anthony.

'Leave it to me, Barrington,' sez he,'leave it all in my hands. You'll have a solicitor on your side, don't forget that, not a solemn-faced numskull like that fellow Fitzsimons. As for Lenahan,' sez he, snappin' his fingers, 'afther the way he's insulted not only me but my whiskey this day, if I get him into the witness-box, damme, I'll riddle him!'

'Witness-box!' sez Mr Barrington. 'Sure you know that a man in a bank can't let this go to witness-boxes. What in the name av heavens is that!' sez he, as there came a most blood-curdlin' yell from upstairs. — 'This is more av Lenahan,' sez he. 'He must have come back. — By the holy poker I'll be hanged for him.'

The three av us ran out into the hall, an' there on the first landin' was a chimley-sweep with his brushes in wan hand an' him holdin' a bag av soot on his shoulder with the other; and' the groans Billy Lenahan had let out av him was nothin' to the gowls av the sweep.

By this time Mr Barrington was near astray in his mind.

'What's wrong with *you*, you fool?' he roars up at the sweep. — 'Do you hear me? What's *wrong* with you? — Oh, sufferin' saints,' — sez he, chargin' up the stairs in a rage, 'can't you answer me?'

But with that the sweep let another whillaloo out av him, an' bent two-double with the pain; an' the bag av soot just emptied itself carefully over Mr Barrington from the crown av his head down. It was the turnin' point with Mr Barrington. He let a roar out av him, dashed the soot out av his eyes, an' gripped the unfortunate sweep by the throat. Down the stairs he trailed him, shakin' the poor divil like a rat, an' along the hall. Then he sent him head-foremost into the street with a hearty toe av his boot an' slammed the hall-door. An' all the time Mr Anthony was at his heels callin' out in desperation:

'He swept the dinin'-room chimney first, Barrington. Mrs Shanks says he swept the dinin'-room chimney first!'

But Mr Barrington give no heed. As he stalked back into the hall he fell on his mouth an' nose over the brushes that the sweep had dhropped. He lepped to his feet with a string av oaths that would have filled a pass-book, grabbed the brushes, tore the door open, an' burst into the street in a cloud av soot, like a train comin' out av a tunnel.

By this time poor wee Mrs Shanks was near in hysterics, between fear an' curiosity.

'But what is it all about, Mr Anthony?' she sez, very pitiful. 'Oh, what *is* it all about?'

'The whole thing is perfectly simple, Mrs Shanks,' sez Mr Anthony, quite bland an' easy, but polishin' away very hard at his eyeglass, to gain time. 'Chimney-sweepin's a dry job; we may have left the sideboard open; the sweep saw our whiskey bottle an' helped himself — liberally. Now Mr Lenahan — the fat gentleman, Mrs Shanks — having complained in the bank to my friend Mr Barrington that he was suffering from what he calls "pains", Mr Barrington told him to come here an' he'd hurry afther him an' give him a little whiskey to cure the pains. When Mr Barrington took out the bottle half the whiskey was gone! He was bewildered. I was bewildered. We smelt soot, but didn't connect it with the theft. But as we left the dining-room afther curing Mr Lenahan Barrington saw a sweep. He put two an' two together at once; an' I may tell you that if it wasn't his good fortune to enjoy the advice av the best solicitor in — in Ireland, begad — they'll add up in the end to considerably more than four, not to speak av costs. — Just place the whiskey back in the sideboard, Mrs Shanks. I want to have a few words on this unfortunate affair with Mr Murphy, upstairs.

'Did you hear me, Pat?' sez he, skippin' round the drawin'-room in great glee. 'On the spur av the moment, mind you — just question an' answer. What a witness I would make! All explained, you see: Lenahan's pains — that they may gripe him to the Day av Judgment!' he threw in, just passin' — 'Mr Barrington's assault, an' the provocation for it — you saw how quickly I spotted that the sweep had been at the whiskey — no mention, you'll observe, av dosings or adulteration ——'

'You're a wonder, Mr Anthony,' sez I; an', troth, it had been quick av him.

'But as neat a stroke as any,' sez he, rubbin' his hands, 'was how I concealed the hidin'-place av the whiskey. Did you notice that, Pat? She'll think it was in the sideboard all the time. An' when our two fresh bottles go to their nest in the chimney to-morrow she'll never be a bit the wiser, nor her son either. — I'm a great man in a tight place, now amn't I? — But what's keepin' Barrington?' sez he, breakin' off an' lookin' at me very serious.

'I hope he hasn't got into any trouble with the polis, Mr Anthony,' sez I. 'He followed up that sweep terrible wicked.'

'Ha!' sez Mr Anthony, brightenin' up again, 'begad he might. The new sergeant's a terror, an' would lift the angel Gabriel for playin' music in the streets. This looks like another bit av professional business, I declare. What a pity there'll be nothin' but honour an' glory out av it for me. — Sit down there, Pat, till I shave. I'll put on my frock-coat, too, just to intimidate the sergeant; an' then we'll be off to the barracks on chance.'

An' you could see by his eye that anythin' Mr Barrington might have committed on the sweep, short av manslaughter, would just be jam to Mr Anthony.

But funny an' all as Mr Anthony's antics were, if I'd only knowed it I was missin' far more fun outside.

I never was clear how much av the doctored whiskey the sweep took, but anyway he knew he had took what didn't belong to him, an' whatever pains he was sufferin' was cured in a twinklin' by the fear he was in av Mr Barrington. The minit he got himself gathered up at the foot av Mrs Shanks's steps away he went like a hare, with his head down, along a lane to his left. But if he did, Mr Gault, the resident magistrate, was walkin', very slow an' pompous, in the opposite direction. The sweep just took him in the middle av the waistcoat; an' the next minit an animal with four legs, an' all four kickin' like blazes, was rollin' over an' over in the road. The sweep had caught Mr Gault to save himself, an' Mr Gault had caught the sweep to keep him from gettin' away, an' by the time the sweep had fought himself free Mr Gault was liker a moultin' magpie nor a resident magistrate, an' the polisman he got hold av in the main street hardly knowed him.

The minit the polisman heard the complaint he out with his baton an' took to his heels. An' it behoved him to. The new sergeant had come down on the town like a blight, an' would have summoned you for suckin' the froth av a bottle av porter off your moustache afther closin' hours. He had chased all the kindly old staff av polis that knowed the capacity av every man in the town within wan glass av whiskey; an' the new bobbies was prowlin' round the streets as hungry for the human race as the lions in a travellin' menagerie.

But by this time it was fallin' dusk; an' with all the zeal in the world a polisman can't see very far with two out av five street lamps burnin' oil, an' the rest burnin' wicks. The constable took a turnin' too soon, an' too quick; an' Mr Barrington, who had took the wrong turnin' himself, got him as full in the face with wan av the sweep's long-handled brushes as if he'd been tiltin' at the sports. There was no time for explainin'. The constable seen the black face, an' gripped Mr Barrington by the throat. Mr Barrington got wan home on the constable's jaw with a wee hand-brush that the sweep kept for cleanin' out flues, before he seen it was the law had him an' gavc in, but not in time to save himself from a welt av the baton that would havc bcat a carpet. Then off he went as quiet as a lamb, thankin' the powers that he was too sooty for the little knot av followers to recognize him. All the time he thought it was for what he had done on the sweep, an' hadn't a vestige av a notion that he was bein' marched to the barracks to be charged with an aggravated assault on the resident magistrate. When it did dawn on him he first av all near burst a blood-vessel with rage, an' then half-massacred the sergeant, an' the constable that had arrested him, tryin' to fight his way out. For he hoped to break away without bein' known, an' then run home an' wash his face for a disguise. Two to wan is big odds, however. In the end the pair were over-many for him, frog-marched him down the passage, an' flung him into the black-hole. An' when he got on his feet an' turned to see what he had fell over, who was it but Billy Lenahan stretched out on the floor sleepin' off the two-thirds av Mr Anthony's bottle av whiskey.

The sergeant, bein' the superior officer, had come pretty well out av the tussle; but the constable had to change his tunic an' stop his nose bleedin'. By the time he got back to his beat he was near due to be relieved. An' as he made his way home to the barracks, now an' then feelin' the tip av his nose very gingerly an' thinkin' out all the fearful things he would swear at the Petty Sessions, here, comin' up the street fornent him at a half-run, was the very man he had threw into the black-hole a short while before! He paused in his step, looked again, in the light av the first lamp that was lit; an' sure enough it was his man, brushes an' all.

'An escape, by the powers!' sez he. He loosened his baton for the second time that day, gave a yell av vengeance, an' the next minit he was tearin' down the middle av the road about twenty yards behind the sweep, afther takin' a flyin' lepp over his brushes that would ha' cleared the water-jump at the Grand National.

For the sweep it was. After he had escaped, first Mr Barrington, an' then the disaster with the resident magistrate, he was on the high-road to leave the town when all at once he minded he hadn't his brushes. What to do about them he did not know. He was afeared to face Mr Barrington, an' still more scared av fallin' into the hands av the polis. An' as he skulked about the streets switherin' in his mind, here doesn't he come out right in front av the polis barracks. All was in peace, an' nobody to be seen. The fight with Mr Barrington was over. The little crowd was melted. The sergeant was restin'; the reliefs was gone out; an' divil a wan had thought av the brushes that was lyin' quite peaceable under the lamp in the front wall av the barracks.

The sweep took a hasty squint round, dashed across the road, boned his brushes, an' off up the road as quick as he thought he could go, till he came back down it again in front av the constable.

The race was over before anybody seen it begin. The sweep was far the lighter av the two on his feet; but breathin' soot an' coal-dust is bad for the bellows. Ten yards past the barracks door the constable ran him down; an' you should have seen that bobby's face as he marched *his* sweep into the guard-room by wan door at the very minit that the sergeant marched *his* wan in from the black-hole by the other!

I seen them both, for Mr Anthony an' I only got to the barracks a couple or three minits before. In his usual way Mr Anthony had simply took charge av the whole concern, an' ordered the prisoners to be brought out av the black-hole; feelin' his way, av course; for he didn't know what had happened. The sergeant hadn't the courage to resist the eyeglass an' the frock-coat; an', as I told you, the two sweeps dead-heated into the guard-room, Billy Lenahan makin' a bad third. Mr Anthony hadn't known what to expect; but what he seen was more than he had expected, an' for a minit he was clean punctured. Then he took in the whole situation — a deal sooner than I did, I'll acknowledge — an' the thought av his own cleverness blew him out to the size av a County Court Judge at the very least.

'This is an outrage,' sez he, glarin' at the sergeant. 'What authority have you for detaining my friend Mr Barrington av the bank like a common criminal?'

'Mr Barrington,' sez the sergeant, gapin' round the room. 'I see no Mr Barrington.'

'*This* is Mr Barrington,' sez Mr Anthony, slapping Mr Barrington on the shoulder till the soot rose out av him in clouds, 'illegally imprisoned by you. Release him at once, sir, or take the consequences.'

But the sergeant had got back his courage by this time, an' was beginnin' to lose his temper.

'I think, Mr Anthony, you're takin' a little too much on you, even for a solicitor,' sez he, purty stiff. 'This man may be Mr Barrington av the bank or Mr Barrington av the chimley, but he's charged with common assault an' assaultin' the polis, an' he'll remain in custody till I get hold av the resident magistrate, an' have a private court held. — Orderly,' sez he, 'go at once for Mr Gault.'

'Do you mean to tell me, sir,' sez Mr Anthony, flyin' into wan av his best Petty Sessions rages, 'that you refuse to release this gentleman —' He lifted his hand again.

'Anthony,' sez Mr Barrington, very vicious, 'if you raise any more soot in my face I'll do time for you.'

'On second thoughts,' sez Mr Anthony to the sergeant, payin' no attention to Mr Barrington, 'on second thoughts, an' just to make it all the hotter for you, I'll wait for the resident magistrate.'

He hadn't long to wait. In through the door bounces Mr Gault himself, lookin' like a sweep in his Sunday clothes, an' behind him a very shamefaced young polis-man. The resident magistrate was easy the angriest man av the whole afthernoon.

'I complain av this man, sergeant,' he splutters, pointin' at the young constable. 'I report him. Confound the fellow, he seized me by the throat at my own gate, an' wanted to arrest me as a sweep. — Damme, sir,' sez he, with the whites av his eyes fair glitterin' against the black av his face, 'do I look like an infernal sweep?'

'Your Honour an' sergeant,' speaks up the poor young fellow, near cryin', 'it was reported to me by a respectable rate-payer av this town that a mad sweep had broke out av the county asylum an' was massacreein' men, women, an' children with a joint av his brush. I spotted the black face in the light av his Honour the resident magistrate's avenue lamp; but I declare to me God I had only laid my finger an' thumb on his wind-pipe when I recognized who it was, an' near fainted away.'

Mr Gault could be pompous enough at times, I know; but there was humour in him, too. He just put back his head an' laughed till his face was like the rivers av Europe with the tears. But when the rest av the misfortunes av the evenin' was unfolded before him, I thought he'd have gone off in an apoplexy.

It was enough for Mr Anthony.

'Your Honour,' sez he, very polite an' respectful, 'if I may venture to say it, we're all friends here. — Now we are, sergeant,' sez he. 'Don't be foolish enough to quarrel with me. You and I may have to scratch each other's backs many a time before you leave this town. You've heard the disasters av my clients, your Honour; with your permission I'll tell you how all the trouble arose.' An' he out all over again with the yarn he had told Mrs Shanks.

'Now I would suggest, your Honour,' sez he, just gettin' well into his stride —

'You would,' sez Mr Gault, a trifle dry. 'But I think you'd better let me take charge while I'm still amused. — Sweep,' sez he, 'if it got about these parts that you went round takin' the soot out av your own throat instead av out av other people's chimneys it wouldn't be good for trade. You'd better lodge no complaint. Mr Barrington, your wrath was righteous, but a little on the severe side. It might help your — your black brother along the path av virtue if you provided him with the means av keeping his throat free av soot for a day or two. Lenahan's case I don't quite understand.'

But Billy was too able to miss his chance.

'Your Honour,' sez he, 'I'd be long sorry to contradict even a solicitor; but you haven't been told the truth, the whole truth, or anythin' like the truth. Mr Anthony an' Mr Barrington have done me an injury this day that I'll not be the better av till my dyin' hour. I *was* invited into your lodgin's, Mr Anthony, as you say; but it was for an ordinary drink, not for rat poison —'

Mr Anthony can't wink except with his eyeglass eye. He turned towards the resident magistrate, an' his eyeglass dhropped.

'As I told you before, Lenahan,' sez Mr Gault, 'I don't quite understand your case. But you were drunk, Lenahan. An' a big powerful fellow like you seldom gets arrested without some kind av a scuffle. — Drunk,' sez Mr Gault, countin' on his fingers, 'assault on the police, a bad record in the matter av illicit spirits. You'll come before *me*, Lenahan —'

'If the two gentlemen'll make up a couple or three quid between them,' sez Billy, who was no dunce, 'I'll not spoil sport.'

The resident magistrate looked at Mr Anthony.

'We'll give the dirty big dog three pounds,' sez Mr Anthony with venom.

'Very well,' sez the resident magistrate. 'You make no charge, then, sergeant?'

'No, your Honour,' sez the sergeant, chokin' on it a bit, all the same.

'Good,' sez Mr Gault, with a wise wee twinkle all round. 'Then I'll go home, an' wash my face.'

'Would you mind leavin' the room for a little, sergeant,' sez Mr Anthony afther the resident magistrate had gone. 'Thank you. An' now, do you, sweep, an' you, Lenahan, go out into the passage.'

He took a couple av sheets av paper out av his pocket an' sat down at the sergeant's desk an' wrote for two or three minits.

'A pound for the sweep, Barrington?' sez he, 'Eh?'

'Two,' sez Mr Barrington. 'I never knew what soot tasted like till to-day.'

'One,' sez Mr Anthony, snappin' his mouth very firm. 'In full settlement av all claims!' he reads out. 'Give him this pound, Pat; an' make him sign the indemnity. If he fell off a chimney an' broke his neck any time these ten years that fellow Lenahan would marry the widow an' blackmail us. Three pounds for that oily ruffian himself, that had the impudence to compare me to a pettifogger like Fitzsimons. He'll change his opinion, I think. Give him this envelope. An', Pat,' sez he, 'here's five shillin's. Hand over to Lenahan an' the sweep in Michael Cassidy's private bar, an' let the fun end where it started. Come up then to Mrs Shanks's. I'm dyin' for my dinner.'

I gave the sweep his money in Michael Cassidy's private room, an' a jorum that would have made ink av a whole bucket av soot, an' sent him off.

'Here,' sez Billy Lenahan holdin' out his hand. 'Where's mine?'

'There it is,' sez I; 'an' I grudge it to you. Three good pounds for wan or two gripes in your inside. You may well snigger.' For he was shakin' like a jelly-fish with the laughin'.

'Will you keep a secret?' sez he. 'It's too good to have all to myself. The three av you followed me from Michael Cassidy's pub this afthernoon, didn't you?'

'I know we did,' sez I.

'I saw you,' sez he.

'Well, what if you did? sez I. 'There's no great secret in that.'

'That isn't the secret,' sez Billy. 'The secret is that I hardly lipped the doctored whiskey at all. Do you think a man that's been makin' potheen as long as I have doesn't know whiskey from medicine? But I think you'll give in, Pat,' sez he, grinnin' all over his face at the recollection, 'that I managed to be purty sick on the little I did take.'

I stood lookin' at him for a minit; an' the scunner riz in me at the rascality an' cuteness av the big porpoise.

'Come on an' have a drink with me out av the profits,' sez Billy, openin' the envelope. 'Maybe that'll bring a smile to your face, you sour ould —' He stopped all at once, an' stood glarin' at Mr Anthony's letter. Then he read it all over again to himself with a look on his face as if it couldn't possibly be true.

'Oh, curse on the little window-eyed son av a dog,' sez he, shakin' his clenched fist in the air. 'May the divil —'

I wouldn't like to set down what Big Billy Lenahan put out av him as he danced round Michael's snug that night.

'Stop it, Billy,' sez I, at the last. 'In the name av the saints what has Mr Anthony said to you?'

I snatched the letter from his hand, an' this is what I read:

> 'Referring to the gratuity of £3 (Three pounds stg) to be given you by my client Mr Barrington at the request of Mr Gault, R.M. — As advised by me my client is applying the said sum of three pounds in reduction of your overdue and unpaid Bill in the Downshire Bank. This course has been taken in your own interests with the object of preventing your being twice drunk at my client's expense on the same day.'

I just opened the door, an' ran. Billy had started again, an' there was no tellin' when Michael Cassidy's whiskey might catch fire.

Mr Anthony was still at his dinner when I went into the dinin'-room.

'Sit down, Pat,' sez he. 'I'm just finished'. I waited a while for Barrington, but he's still scrapin' himself. You did that little job?'

'Mr Anthony,' sez I, 'all I have to tell you is that the man that said Mr Fitzsimons was cleverer nor you knows more about it now than he did.'

Contrary to his usual Mr Anthony didn't begin to make a song about himself — but looked at me very serious an' calm.

'Pat,' sez he, 'no matter how clever a man is — an' av course I'll give in I'm no dunce — there are times when things run awkward with him, an' he doesn't get showin' his abilities to the full. This afthernoon I was fortunate. From the very first threatenin' av disaster till what I take the liberty av callin' the triumphant conclusion, everythin' turned out well in my hands. I've sat on the sergeant; I've pleased the R.M.; I've got my friend Barrington out av a nasty hole; I've taught Mr William Lenahan the difference between low cunnin' an' — an' genius; I've given an unfortunate divil av a sweep a lesson, an' still dealt with him in a Christian manner; an' now at the end av a successful but very tiring day,' sez he, bowin' a bit old-fashioned to Mrs Shanks, 'owing to the unconscionable extent av my friend Barrington's ablutions I've been rewarded with two helps av my favourite Christmas pudding.'

'I would have showed no Christianity to thon sweep, Mr Anthony,' sez Mrs Shanks, puttin' down her tray, 'afther the hole he made in the whiskey. — I declare to you there was just barely enough left in the bottle to make sauce for your puddin'.'

Mr Anthony looked at her. He said nothin'; but he turned white; an' I could see him grippin' the edge av the table with his two hands.

'Is *that* it?' sez he, in a half-whisper. 'Is *that* what it is? An' I thought it was because I took the second help av puddin'. — Run, Pat,' he groans out, 'run for the doctor! — Barrington, Mrs Shanks; get Barrington! — I'm dyin', I'm dyin', an' my will not made. *A—h!'* He let a screech out av him, an' doubled up' with his head on the table. As I ran out av the room I seen that his eyeglass had fell into the sauce-boat. But Mr Anthony didn't care.

Dear Ducks

Wee Mr Anthony the solicitor, was wan av them men that hasn't room in their heads for more than wan idea at a time. Him bein' a solicitor, ye might think it was law his head was full av; but not a bit av it. Outside av his own office or the Petty Sessions Court, law never troubled him; he just passed his final examination an' then placed the whole business in the hands av the divil. Sport was his weakness. In the summer he played tennis as if he made his livin' by it; an' it was well for him he didn't, for with him bein' so short-sighted he stopped a deal more balls with the pit av his stomach then ever he did with his bat. But with the end av the good weather he dhropped the tennis like a hot potato an' took to the shootin'. An' then the Coroner sharpened his pencil; for when Mr Anthony turned out a charge av shot on the world only an all-seein' Providence could tell where some av the pickles would come to a full stop.

I was standin' whettin' my scythe wan October evenin' when Mr Anthony comes into the yard. 'Pat,' sez he, 'is there any wild-duck about that a body could shoot handy?'

'Lashins av them,' sez I. 'Do you want a brace or two?'

'I do,' sez he. 'The fact is, Pat,' he goes on, 'Miss Livingston an' I is a bit friendly lately——'

'Oh, well,' sez I, 'what odds? If it comes to a breach av promise you can conduct your own defence.'

'I haven't got the length av a promise yet,' sez he, 'let alone a breach av it.'

'What's holdin' ye?' sez I, 'that can talk round a whole bench av magistrates, let alone an innocent slip av a girl that might be your daughter.'

'You're a liar,' sez Mr Anthony; 'I'm not even ten years older than her. — It's the shootin' is holdin' me back,' sez he. 'She's clean death on my takin' up a gun; an' I'd as soon live single all my life as give it up now that I have masthered it.'

'Masthered it, God forgive ye!' sez I to myself — an' then out loud: 'There's no doubt you've come on extraordinary well at it this last winter or two.'

'Haven't I, Pat?' sez he, all pleased. 'Haven't I now? D'ye mind that grouse I shot, last June was a year?'

'Wheesht! Mr Anthony,' sez I.

'I don't care a fig,' sez he. 'Close season, or no close season, didn't the bird rise up fornent me an' just ask for it? I never made a prettier shot in my life. Blast it, why wasn't it in the month av August, when I could have told people? But that's neither here nor there,' sez he. 'It's in my mind to shoot a couple av nice ducks an' send them round to Miss Livingston. If she had a wing an' a bit av the breast av wan av them sittin' before her on a plate, she might think betther av my shootin'.'

'Does she not think well av it, as it is?' sez I.

'Well,' sez Mr Anthony, lookin' a wee bit foolish, 'there was an accident happened to me wan day lately when I was walkin' across the fields with her. A rabbit got up in front av us, an' I fired a bit hasty an' missed it.'

'Is that all?' sez I. 'She surely wouldn't expect even you to hit everything you fire at.'

'It wasn't that,' sez Mr Anthony, rubbin' his chin. 'The fact is, Pat,' sez he, 'I hit her dog. It was that blasted wee Pomeranian, that goes along with its tail arched over its back as if it was as proud av its hind-end as it is av its face; an' av course in the tail it got it. Curse the misbegotten little brute, if it carried its tail decently out behind it like an ordinary dog the divil a pickle it would ha' got, an' I might even have killed the rabbit. However, that's past prayin' for now. Where do you think I could get a pair av ducks?'

'Try the marshy ground where the Ballygullion river flows into lake,' sez I. 'It's clean alive with ducks, an' most av them flappers, an' flyin' very slow.'

'Flyin' slow,' sez Mr Anthony, a bit vexed. 'Flyin' slow, is it? What do I care whether they're flyin' slow or fast. You'd think I was a novice to hear you talkin'.' An' off he goes in a huff.

But about three days afther, back he comes again, an' not near as cocky this time.

'Did she like the ducks?' sez I.

'I always thought this tennis playin' was bad for a man's shootin',' sez

Mr Anthony. 'Would you believe it, Pat, but I've been down at the marshes these three evenin's, an' fired away as many cartridges as would fill a counsellor's wig, an' the divil a feather I've brought down.'

'Did ye not as much as wound somethin'?' sez I, chaffin' him.

'Well,' sez he, 'there *was* wan, a drake, I think, that flew away very slow an' heavy afther I fired at him.'

'I wouldn't think much av that,' sez I. 'He might have a touch av rheumatism, sleepin' in the damp. You'll have to take another evenin' or two at them.'

'It's no good,' sez he, 'till I get this infernal tennis out av my system. Besides, I haven't time. There's a dinner-party at Mr Livingston's on Friday, an' I wanted the ducks for that.'

'Ye needn't bother your head,' sez I. 'My wife has a pair av young ones fattened for them.'

'Has she?' sez he, lookin' disappointed; 'that's a pity. Pat,' sez he, all excited, 'would she sell them to me? Hold your tongue, now. Let her send word to the Livingstons that the rats ate them; an' then I'll come along with a pair just in the nick av time. Don't talk to me,' sez he, hoppin' round as the notion took hold av him, 'there's not a bein' about the place would know a duck from a wather-hen, barrin' Mr Livingston himself, an' sure they'll be plucked clean naked before they get his length.'

'Ye've no sense, Mr Anthony,' sez I. 'Wouldn't the very scullery-maid know when a bird had its throat cut instead av bein' shot?'

'So she would,' sez Mr Anthony. 'That's awkward. — Wait now,' sez he; 'I'm not beat yet. Dhrive them through the gap in the hedge there, one at a time, an' I'll shoot them as they come through. What about that, eh? It's hard to get the betther av me, mind ye, when I lay my brains to a thing. Go on, now, an' get them. What are ye waitin' for?'

'It's clean murdher, Mr Anthony,' sez I, 'forbye that ye might miss them.'

'Miss them!' sez he. 'Miss them, ye imperent ould vagabond. An' them walkin'! Didn't ye see me bringin' down a woodcock in the Drumnaquirk wood only last February?'

'I did,' sez I; 'but you were aimin' at a wood-pigeon at the time. — However, I suppose I'll have to be as big a fool as yourself. Away an' post yourself, an' I'll dhrive in the ducks. What size av shot are ye usin'?'

'Number three,' sez he.

'It's too big,' sez I. 'Ye'll damage them.'

'It's all I have,' sez he. 'I've killed ducks with it before.'

'Ye have,' sez I; 'an' ye killed a terrier dog av mine with it, too. If Mr Livingston breaks wan av them gold teeth av his on a pickle av number three shot, I wouldn't give much for your chance av marryin' his daughter. But have your own way. Ye'll have it anyway, I know.'

So off I goes an' brings the two ducks, an' them quackin' away as if they'd ten years to live. Ye'd ha' thought somebody had told them what sort av a shot Mr Anthony was. When I came back he was on the far side av the gap with the gun in his hand.

'Are ye ready, now?' sez I. 'Here's the first av them.'

'Hold on a minit,' sez he — an' I could tell by his voice he was flusthered — 'I want a good steady shot. I'm going to lie down on my belly.'

'If wan av them two-year-old bullocks av mine steps on ye, ye'll get up again,' sez I. — 'Bless my soul,' sez I to myself as a thought struck me; an' I ran over to the gap an' peeped through. It was well I looked at Mr Anthony first. If I hadn't ha' shouted, I was a dead man.

'Good Heavens, Pat!' sez he, lowerin' the gun, 'I thought it was wan av the ducks.'

'Ye didn't think a duck had a pair av nailed boots on it, did ye?' sez I. 'Ye'll do ten years for manslaughter, yet — I wanted to make sure the bullocks was out av your line av fire.'

'Will ye dhrive out them d——d ducks an' have done with it?' sez Mr Anthony in a rage. 'Ye have my nerve near ruined as it is.'

'Come on, then,' sez I. 'Blaze away!'

I whished the first av them through the gap, keepin' well to the rear myself, I may tell ye. There came a terrible roar av a report. When I run through the gap there was as much smoke dhriftin' down the field as if the kitchen chimney was on fire, an' Mr Anthony rowlin' over an' over in the middle av it, an' cursin' most lamentable.

'In the name av goodness, Mr Anthony,' sez I, 'what's wrong? Did ye shoot out av the wrong end av the gun?' For, troth, he was capable av it.

'It was you, ye ould fool ye,' sez he, risin' to his feet an' rubbin' himself. 'Ye had me scared into thinkin' I might miss the beast, an' I pulled the two triggers at the wan time. My backbone is out av joint,' sez he, reachin' round between his shouldher-blades. 'But I'll go bail I killed the duck, anyway.'

'Where is it, then, if ye did?' sez I, lookin' all round. For there was no duck to be seen.

'It's the most extraordinary thing,' sez Mr Anthony, stickin' the eye-glass in his eye an' looking all round him. 'I'll swear, an' kiss the book, that I hit it.'

'I'll tell ye what ye've done,' sez I, 'ye've blew it to pieces.' An' that's what he *had* done. We searched up an' we searched down, but divil at all we ever discovered av the same duck but the neb an' wan av the feet.

'Aw, well,' sez I, at the last, 'it had a lovely death, even if there isn't much eatin' about the carcass. Will I dhrive out the other wan for ye, now?'

'Dhrive it to hell if ye like,' sez Mr Anthony, fair boilin' over. 'Have ye any whiskey about the place? — Then, come an' rub my shoulder with some av it. — An' ye may throw that blasted gun in the well,' sez he, an' stalks off into the house.

But by the time his shoulder was well rubbed with the whiskey, an' him had a good jorum av it in his inside, he began to come round.

'Say what ye like, Pat,' sez he, 'it was a great shot. Plumb in the middle I must ha' got that duck.'

'Ye must have,' sez I, sootherin' him. 'It was only outlyin' bits like the neb that was found. There's no doubt ye have a very straight eye.'

'Haven't I, Pat?' sez he, swellin' himself out. 'Haven't I now? — Curse that tennis,' sez he; 'if I had let it alone an' practised with the gun all summer, I could shoot midges by now. — Look here,' sez he, 'I'll send Miss Livingston that brace av wild-duck yet. They'll be late for the dinner-party, but what matter?'

'They needn't be,' sez I. 'Couldn't ye come out to-morrow evenin' to the marshes?'

'I can't,' sez he. 'The Quarther Sessions is on. It's a pity too, an' me shootin' the way I am. But I'm prosecutin' in some poachin' cases, an' I must turn up. — But wait, Pat,' sez he; 'the ducks'll be plentier in a week or two, won't they?'

'With the first touch av frost,' sez I. 'There'll be dhroves av them.'

'Very well,' sez he, 'the next likely evenin' that ye see any plenty av ducks in the marshes, send for me an' I'll come should it be rainin' conveyances an' snowin' wills. I've got the true knack av shootin', this time. Give me the neb av the duck, till I show it to my articled clerk. — Ye'll not forget, now, to send me word.'

So I promised I would not; an' clean forgot all about it till a fortnight aftherwards when I was out myself lookin' for ducks with the old muzzle-loader, an' Big Billy Lenahan av the Hills with me. It was a fine frosty evenin', with just enough ice about to fetch the ducks to the open water, an' I knowed there'd be strings av them coming down the river presently.

'Billy,' sez I, 'this is just the very night for Mr Anthony. I must send him word.'

An' then I remembered I was makin' a mistake.

'Let him stay at home, the wee gas-bag,' sez Billy, with a growl. 'Five pounds his long tongue cost me at the Quarther Sessions; bad luck to him.'

'If ye let yourself be caught poachin', Billy,' sez I, 'ye needn't blame Mr Anthony. He's prosecutin' solicitor, an' he has his duty to do.'

'I know he has,' sez Billy, 'but he needn't have done it that wicked. He promised me he wouldn't press the case; an' then he goes an' gets himself all blew up with his own talk, an' I'm fined five pounds through him, the vain wee cockatoo. — But take your time,' sez Billy, 'I'll be even with him yet.'

'Ach, don't bear malice, Billy,' sez I. 'There's no harm in Mr Anthony.'

'There's a deal too much av the blether about him in a law court,' sez Billy, still very sour. 'He's all gab and guts, like a young crow. But let him come. We'll have some fun out av him, anyway.'

So we sent wan av the young Robinsons for Mr Anthony, an' Billy an' I went on afther the ducks. In about half an hour's time he come up behind us, an' him an almighty swell with a fur-lined coat an' his evenin'-dhress below it.

'You're never goin' to shoot ducks in that rig, Mr Anthony?' sez I.

'I am not,' sez he, 'worse luck. I'm going out to dine at Miss Armytage's av the Hall. Have ye shot many?'

'Half a dozen, up till now,' sez I; 'but they'll be comin' along thicker presently.'

'Well, bad cess to it,' sez Mr Anthony, very savage. 'An' just the evenin' I can't get at them. You'd think they knew they were safe.'

'Away home an' change your clothes,' sez I, 'an' send Miss Armytage word you're not well.'

'I can't,' sez he, bitin' at his nails; 'no, hang it, I can't. Miss Livingston is to be there. Between you an' me, Pat,' sez he, 'I've given her a hint that I'm going to ask her a question to-night. — But do you an' Billy go on, an' I'll walk with you. I've been readin' up about duck-shootin' since I saw you, an' I might be able to give ye a wrinkle or two.'

'Come on, then,' sez I. For I seen some very offensive expressions thremblin' on Billy Lenahan's tongue.

A couple av minutes later along comes a pair av ducks just barely within range, an' I fetched the near wan down.

'If ye'd waited till the two av them was in line,' sez Mr Anthony, 'the wan shot would have killed both.'

'If you could fly afther them, you could catch them with your hands,' sez Billy, very sour. 'It's a pity it's not you is carryin' the gun.'

'I wish I was,' sez Mr Anthony. 'Bad cess to it, I wish I was. I could shoot tonight, I know I could. An' look at the strings av ducks comin' along there, far out. Where's that old pair av wadin' boots I gave you, Pat? If you were only out in the middle there you could shoot rings round you. — Pat,' sez he, dancin' round with excitement, 'away home for them, quick. Damme, I'll put them on an' have a shot myself. Run; an' don't waste a minit. I must turn up at the dinner. My whole future life might depend on in. But I'd like to have a couple av shots before I commit myself to matrimony. There's no telling what effect marriage might have on my shootin'. Away with you now, quick.'

'Ye'd betther wait till you're coming back from the dinner, Mr Anthony,' sez I. 'The moon'll be up by then.'

'There'll be two moons up by then,' sez Mr Anthony. 'Did you ever taste Miss Armytage's port wine? — Go on an' get the boots. Gimme your gun an' the powder an' shot. I'll be loadin' the empty barrel while you're away.'

'Betther let Billy load it,' sez I. 'You have no great experience with a muzzle-loader.'

'Blethers,' sez Mr Anthony, layin' hold av the gun, 'you'd think I was a beginner to hear you talkin'. I blew the nail off my thumb with a muzzle-loader before Billy was born.'

'Keep an eye on him while he's chargin' her,' sez I to Billy in an undhertone, 'only if you're wise it'll be from behind a tree. I'll be back before he has time to shoot much more than the dog.' An' off I went, hot-foot; for I knowed there would be fun before the evenin' was over.

When I got back he was sittin' on a stone in his stocking-feet, waitin'.

'In the name av goodness what kept ye all this time,' sez he. 'The toes is near froze off me. An' there's not less than five hundhred ducks gone past us. — Here, pull the boots on me, the pair av you, an' I'll lean on the gun.'

'If ye fill the muzzle av that gun wi' dirt, Mr Anthony,' sez I, 'all ye'll kill this evenin' 'll be a solicitor; for the charge'll come through the near end av her.'

'Blast it,' sez he, in a splutther, 'am I doin' that? — Wait a minit, an' I'll lean on the butt.'

'Well, if you think I'm goin to pull on your boots with the muzzle av a loaded gun proddin' me in the small av the back, you're mistaken,' sez Billy. 'I'll hold him, Pat, an' do you pull. — There you are. Away ye go, now; straight in front av you.'

'Where are ye sendin' the man, Billy?' sez I. 'Come back, Mr Anthony. You're headin' right for the main dhrain; an' if ye go in there it's a submarine ye'll need instead av wadin' boots. — Keep to your left. — Easy now; don't fire! That's only a coot scutterin' along the top av the wather. Wade as far out as the boots'll let ye. The ducks is frightened av us on the bank here.'

'Bad manners to you anyway, with your main dhrain,' sez he. 'You've shaken my nerve. How will I know the main dhrain if I come on it?'

'You'll know by goin' in over your ears,' sez I. 'But you're not headin' that way now.'

So off he moves through the wather an' mud, going very cautious.

'Why didn't ye let him go on the way he was goin,' sez Billy. 'There'll be no sport with him now.'

'I never seen him go out with a gun yet that there wasn't sport,' sez I. 'He'll shoot somethin' he oughtn't to before he goes home; take care it isn't yourself, ye black-hearted ruffian. — Wait; here he's comin' back. What has he done now? Listen to the language av him. — What's wrong, Mr Anthony?'

'It's them cursed coots,' sez he. 'The wather was just lippin' up to the top av the boots when a couple av them came splattherin' by, makin' a wake like a steamer; an' there's about two gallon av mud gone down the legs av my evenin'breeches. An' the moths has ate the seat out av the only spare pair I have. Confound it, anyway,' sez he, 'I may stay at home now.'

'Such nonsense,' sez I. 'Won't your feet be undher the table. If it was your shirt-front was round your legs you might be talkin'. — Hurry up an' try a shot. The light's goin'.'

'I might as well let it alone,' sez he; 'I'm goin' to have no luck to-night. But I'll have a try, seein' I'm here.' An' off he wades again.

'It's the first time I ever went out with him,' sez I to Billy, 'that he wasn't cock-sure he'd fill his game-bag with wan shot. It's a good sign. He'll hit somethin' to-night, see if he doesn't. — Do ye think he loaded that second barrel all right?'

'He did,' sez Billy. 'I kept a careful eye on him. Just a fair charge he put in, an' no more.'

'Watch him, then, Billy,' sez I, 'till we see how he does —— Juke down! There's a string av ducks comin' between us an' him. — He doesn't see them, the wee donkey. Shout to him, Billy.'

'No, don't shout,' sez Billy. 'There's some beyond him as well. — Is he never goin' to shoot?' sez he, fidgin'. I could see Billy was near as excited as myself. 'He sees them,' chuckles he. 'Look out for fun now.'

Up goes Mr Anthony's gun to his shoulder. He followed the ducks with the muzzle till I was near bursted with holdin' my breath. I could see him bracin' himself up as he pulled the trigger.

'Now for a shower av ducks, Billy,' sez I.

There came nothing but the crack av a cap.

'Bad luck to it,' sez I, 'a missfire. I knowed he wouldn't load her right. — Behind you, Mr Anthony!' I shouts, leppin' up. 'Behind ye!'

He wheeled half-round at the sound av my voice, seen the second lot av ducks, up with the gun again, an' fired. There was a report like the blastin' av a quarry. Mr Anthony staggered back, recovered himself a bit, clawin' in the air, an' then souse down he went on the broad av his back, an' disappeared.

'Quick, Billy,' shouts I; 'follow me. He'll be dhrowned! He's in the main dhrain.'

'Easy,' sez Billy, quite cool, layin' hold av my arm. 'He's fifty yards from the main dhrain. There he is on his feet again. Oh, great Christopher,' sez he, beginning' to laugh, 'will ye look at him!'

An', troth though I was heart-sorry for the wee man, I could hardly keep my own face straight. It was just like wan av them sea lions bobbin' up and out av a tank at the circus, only instead of havin' a sealskin coat on him he was one solid mass av mud an' glar. He turned round a couple av times, gropin' in front of him with his hands, an' then he started off straight for the main dhrain.

'This way, Mr Anthony,' I calls out, when I could find my voice. 'Come this way.'

He started to come towards the voice, all the time gropin' with his hands, an' wandherin' here an' there as if he was playin' blind-man's buff, an' at last he made the land. The only feature ye could make out in his face was his mouth, an' only that because he kept spittin' out mud an' bits av bullrushes.

'What happened to you at all, at all, Mr Anthony?' sez I, when we got him a sort of a way cleaned. 'Did you trip on anything?'

'Take me home,' he splutthers, 'take me home out av this. An' send word to Miss Armytage that I'm dying av typhoid. I will be, too, before breakfast-time to-morrow,' sez he, spittin out another mouthful av mud. 'There's as much sewage gone down my throat as would give typhoid to a carrion-crow. — It was all that d——d old blunderherbuss of yours. I can handle an ordinary fowlin'-piece with anybody,' sez he, 'an' well you know it; but I won't undhertake to stand up against the kick av a field-gun. By Heavens, it has a recoil like a howitzer! Take me home, I tell ye; and' if ye ever dig that old infernal machine out av the marsh where it's lyin' this minit, by this an' by that I'll be hanged for ye.'

An' not another word could we get out av him till we helped him into his own hall, afther persuadin' the housekeeper that it *was* him.

I walked down the road with Billy, thinkin' very hard, an' every now an' then takin' a look at his face. But he was as solemn as a judge.

'Look here, Billy,' sez I, 'tell me the truth. Did Mr Anthony put only a fair charge into the empty barrel av that gun?'

'He put a fair charge in,' sez Billy. 'The only thing I wasn't quite sure av at the time,' sez he, backin' away from me a step or two, 'was whether he was puttin' it into the empty barrel.'

I suppose I shouldn't ha' done it; but afther a minit or so I sat down beside Billy, an' laughed till I minded that it was my gun that was lyin' at the bottom av the marsh.

Turkey and Ham

When wee Mr Anthony the solicitor was coortin' Mr Livingston's daughter, Miss Betty, he had only the wan trouble. It wasn't his girl; she was a quiet simple affectionate slip av a grey-eyed girl, an' thought the sun riz an' set on him. The bother was, Mr Anthony was so pleased about it that he begun to put on fat. He told me his trouble, one day we were out shootin' over the Bermingham estate, that Miss Betty's father was agent for; an' I only laughed at him.

'What odds does it make,' sez I, 'if your young lady takes no notice?'

That comforted him for a while; but the followin' week a thunderbolt fell on him.

'George,' sez Miss Betty to him wan evenin', very timid, 'I'm thinkin' av tryin' to slim. It would never do for the two av us to get fat,' sez she. 'People would look afther us as we went down the street.'

Mr Anthony jumped as if he had touched an electric wire.

'That settles it,' sez he. 'I needed that jog. Not that I'm greedy, dear; but I'm a great judge av food and wine, and it seemed a pity not to exercise my talent. Now, my mind is made up. As from the end av tonight's dinner — I'll have to eat that, since it's cooked — I go on a diet till I've lost a stone and a half. I will not have you slimming, Betty. Curse it,' sez he, 'I don't care if you grow as round as a dumpling. I love you. But we mustn't become ridiculous. Listen to me, darling,' he sez, warmin' up; 'from tonight I go on to Dr Thompson's diet. It's a corker, mind you. It slimmed old Mrs McGimpsey till she rattled in her coffin; and it may kill me, too; but my word is my oath. Damme, if it wasn't boiled chicken and bacon I'd give tonight's dinner to the dog.'

'Don't overdo it, George,' sez Miss Betty, a trifle frightened. 'You might injure your health. And you forget that tomorrow's Christmas Day, and you're dining with us.'

'I was doing more than that,' sez Mr Anthony. 'I was dining in the middle av the day as well, just to spite my old housekeeper. She has my Christmas dinner bought, a turkey and a ham, and sausages and chestnuts and heaven knows what; and I got a present av two bottles av champagne from Mr Bermingham — the Widow Clicquot, 1921 — that would make a tombstone angel play jazz tunes.'

'But George, darling,' sez Miss Betty, 'were you going to eat and drink all that? And I was sympathizing about your figure!'

'Confound it, no,' sez Mr Anthony. 'I never get anything but a morsel, a couple av slices av breast, and maybe a wing and a sausage or two; and then off goes the rest to her relations. She has a sister married to the gamekeeper av the Bermingham estate, and another to the keeper av the back lodge-gate, and you'd think she was married to them herself. They get about two-thirds av all the food I pay for; and now they're going to get the whole av my Christmas dinner.'

'But it's a shame,' sez Miss Betty, 'an imposition!'

Mr Anthony stopped on the road.

''Gad,' sez he, 'I never thought av that. It *is* an imposition. I've been weak, Betty,' sez he, 'and that's not like me. I can't eat my Christmas dinner — grapefruit and toast, the doctor's diet says — and I can't drink my Christmas champagne; but, begad, if I fast the housekeeper's relatives may fast, too. Pat Murphy's coming round this evening afther dinner to fix up some shooting for St Stephen's Day. I'll give my dinner to him. Not a word!' sez he. 'I want to show you that you're getting a man that loves you better than his meals. It's a point av honour with me, now. Damme,' sez he, 'I'll stick to the diet should I go up the aisle with you, and the people looking through me as if I was a rainbow.'

But when Mr Anthony offered me the dinner that evening it was far too late.

'I just daren't take it, Mr Anthony,' sez I. 'We have a turkey av my wife Mollie's rearin' that she cried over when she was killin' it, as if it was a child; an' the least I can do is to attend the funeral. An' as for the champagne, I wouldn't have the wee bubbles out av my system before the New Year. Eat an' drink the whole lot yourself,' sez I. 'Miss Betty'll never know.'

'I wouldn't do that,' sez Mr Anthony. 'Is it deceive poor Betty even before I married to her? Never!' sez he. 'I'm a man av principle. Beyond what the doctor's diet permits — not a crumb,' sez he, 'not the pop av a cork. I suppose the housekeeper's clan will have to get the dinner afther all.'

'Give it to some decent poor family,' sez I. 'It'll be a friendly turn. An' if a solicitor's soul *can* be saved it may do somethin' in that direction as well.'

'Tell me the name av a family,' sez he, 'and if the champagne goes to heads unaccustomed to anythin' but porter, damme, I'll defend them myself.'

'The O'Greens av Creel's Row are decent people that would be glad av an extra bit an' sup on a day like that,' sez I; 'but, sure, if you sent your Christmas dinner to a Nationalist family there'd be a revolution.'

'This is where brains and experience come in,' sez Mr Anthony, all pleased with himself. 'There's an Orange family called Williamson on the far side av the Row. We'll split the dinner between the two families, an' I'll throw in a dhrop av whiskey, each, to warm their stomachs afther the champagne.'

'If you do that,' sez I, 'your soul an' body are safe for the Christmas holidays, anyway. But if your whiskey is so plenty could you not spare me a dhrop, now?'

'I can,' sez he, 'and will.'

He took down a bottle an' filled out about half a glass.

'Isn't it an extraordinary thing, Pat,' sez he, twirlin' the glass in his hand, 'the way people let drink get a hold av them. Now here I am,' sez he, takin' a sip, 'that have given up this stuff maybe for ever, and I don't care a fig. There's nothin' to give up,' sez he, takin' another sup. 'I've lost the taste for it already. Bless my soul!' he sez emptyin' down the last dhrop, 'I've dirtied your glass. Wait till I get another.'

'All the same, Mr Anthony,' sez I, 'you'll find it a long Christmas day.'

'It can't be helped,' sez he, lookin' a bit glum. 'Principle is principle. But, do you know, Pat; I think it would be a kindly act if you and I dhropped round to the houses av these two poor fellows to-morrow. They'd like to see the giver av the feast; and it might console me undher the diet if I saw other people doing themselves harm instead av me.'

'I'm with you,' sez I, 'if you'll make it early. We're not eatin' our dinner till four. The brother-in-law an his wife are comin' down on the afther-noon train from Belfast.

'Good,' sez Mr Anthony. 'What time do these unfortunate people dine?'

'They don't dine at all,' sez I. 'As soon as the grub is cooked they eat it.'

'Very well,' sez Mr Anthony. I'll not be up myself; but I'll tell the housekeeper to send the stuff about ten. And three hours will cook a ham.'

'It doesn't take near as long to cook drink,' sez I.

'We'll have to take our chance av that,' sez Mr Anthony. 'I can put a flask in my pocket. Let us say half-past twelve at Johnston's corner. Oh, just a minute,' says he. He tossed up a shilling. 'The turkey goes to the O'Greens, and the ham to the Williamsons. We'll call on the Williamsons first; to accustom me to the smell av food. If I encounter the turkey first I might be tempted to taste the stuffing. Don't be surprised if you find me thinner in the morning, Pat. There'll be nothing in me but half a grape-fruit and some kind av sawdust toast. Curse that doctor fellow,' sez he, forgettin' himself a little. 'And to think that he'll be eating bacon and eggs.'

The next day about a quarter to one o'clock Mr Anthony an' I walked up the path to Robert Williamson's cottage. About six feet away from the door Mr Anthony stopped me.

'Do you smell it, Pat?' sez he.

'What?' sez I; afther a hard sniff.

'The ham,' sez he. 'Pure Limerick. I would know it a mile away. They're a queer lot in the South av Ireland, but damme, they can make ham. Lovely,' sez he, takin' a sniff himself. 'I feel well paid already for my little bit av self-sacrifice. Don't let me stay too long. That smell is making me ravenous.'

When we went into the Williamson's kitchen there was nobody there but Mrs Williamson, an' the two children. The fire was barely in, an' there wasn't even a saucepan on it. Mrs Williamson was blowin' the bellows; and' she looked up all surprised. Mr Anthony stammered a little.

'I was just taking a Christmas morning walk with my friend Pat Murphy,' sez he; 'and we thought we'd call and wish you a Happy Christmas.'

'Thank you, sir,' sez Mrs Williamson, well pleased, 'you were always very kind. Shake hands with the gentleman,' sez she to the children, 'and say "Thank you".'

It's very hard to have a child sayin' 'Thank you' for nothin'. Mr Anthony put his hand in his pocket an' fetched out some silver. I looked, an' the divil a thing smaller was among it than two-shillin' bits. He gave the children wan apiece; but you could see by his face he was addin' it to the cost av the ham.

Mrs Williamson thanked him herself with the tears in her eyes.

'The boss got half a day's work this mornin' at double pay,' sez she, 'an' he'll not be back till half-past two, so I haven't a bite cooked in the house that I could offer you.'

Mr Anthony's face fell, an' he gave a very straightforward sniff. Mrs Williamson took the hint.

'You've said it, sir,' sez she. 'It's a bit on the elderly side, sure enough; but maybe you would take a morsel.'

She went to the cupboard an' fetched out a piece av very broadminded-lookin' cheese; though the green was beginnin' to get the better av the Orange.

'Try a piece av that an' a sup av whiskey, sir,' sez she, 'you an' Pat Murphy; just for the credit av the house.'

Mr Anthony turned his back on the cheese, an' filled himself out a stiffish glass. It pulled him together a good deal, for he faced round manful again.

'Thank you, mem,' sez he; 'but I'm on a diet, and cheese is specially forbidden. But you're right to eat that piece at half-past two; for I doubt it will be past its best by three o'clock. — Now don't be drinking all the woman's whiskey, Pat,' sez he to me, that was barely takin' a poor man's drink. 'I thought we were neither to eat nor wet our lips till we got home.'

But I lingered a minute to speak to Mrs Williamson.

'You should have thanked him for the dinner,' sez I. "He's not well pleased.'

'What dinner?' sez she, gapin' at me.

'It was half his dinner was sent you this mornin',' sez I. 'He's on a diet, an' didn't want the good food wasted. A whole Limerick ham, an' whiskey an' champagne wine. Did you not open the parcel yet?'

'If there was a parcel sent me it must have gone astray,' sez she; 'for as true as I'm here I never got a crumb.'

'That's queer,' sez I. 'The housekeeper was to send it — half to you an' half to the O'Greens.'

Mrs Williamson looked very hard at me, an' the colour riz in her face.

'Oh, "fare ye well, Killeavey",' sez she. 'That's all we'll ever hear av it. The ould faggot,' sez she. 'Not that I would give offence to anybody av your persuasion, Mr Murphy; but I expect she has gone an' sent the whole jing-bang to the O'Greens because they're her own sort. Run away, dear!' she sez to the little boy that was hangin' round her. 'Not a word, mind you, to Mr Anthony. I'll say nothin' to my man. He'd want to stand on his rights; an' there's no use havin' a row between neighbours on this av all days in the year. But it's not very Christmas behaviour av her, I'll say that. An' I haven't tasted a bit av Limerick ham since I was at service in the Berminghams! Never mind, Mr Murphy. It's not your fault. But there'll no blessin' follow it.'

I suppose the whiskey did all the better work on Mr Anthony on account av him bein' near empty; but when I caught up on him it was beginning to lift his heart a little.

'Now not one syllable out av you,' sez he, 'about the teaspoonful av whiskey I had. If that cheese wasn't an excuse for at least half a pint I'll go back and eat the stuff. Isn't it a pity we went into the house at all? If I hadn't this cold in my head I'd have smelt it at the gate. Are we near the O'Greens?'

'It's somewhere about this part av the Row,' sez I. 'Take a sniff an' try if you can smell a turkey.'

'There's Mrs O'Green just gone into the door,' sez he, very hasty. 'Come on. I don't want the neighbours to think I'm serving a writ. You haven't four sixpences for a two-shilling piece, Pat, have you? No? Curse it,' sez he, 'I must have put in my pocket the money I had for the Bermingham servants instead av what I got for the poor. How many young O'Greens are there?'

'Seven,' sez I, 'an' three dead.'

'Thank heavens,' sez Mr Anthony. 'I mean for the three dead. My goodness,' sez he, fishing among his change, 'this is going to cost me fifteen-and-sixpence. Can they walk?' lookin' at me with a bit av hope in his eye.

'There's two av them can't, Mr Anthony,' sez I; 'but I doubt they could hold on tight enough to a couple av two-shillin' bits if they were put in their hand.'

'D——n them,' sez he, good-natured enough. 'But I'll give the Berminghams' butler sixpence, and have my revenge.'

Mr and Mrs O'Green an' the seven children were all in the wee kitchen; an' the five that could walk fell on Mr Anthony an' near tore him to bits.

'An' very kind av you, sir,' shouts Mrs O'Green through the noise. 'You were always gentry, Mr Anthony, an' had somethin' in the heel av your hand for the poor man; an' God bless you an' the purty girl you're goin' to marry, an' may you raise as hearty an' healthy a flock as my own an' as many av them, though I doubt the mistress is a bit light in the make for it.'

Mr Anthony had been holdin' on to his money so far; but this was too much for him. He hauled out the silver, an' in his splutther began at the half-crown end, an' cost himself an extra sixpence. There was great enthusiasm; an' Mr Anthony's Sunday breeches aged six months in about three minutes.

'We're just goin' to have our Christmas dinner,' roars Mrs O'Green. 'You'll have a bite with us. Hold on till I try the pot.'

'Good gracious,' sez Mr Anthony in my ear, 'I hope they haven't put in the champagne, too.'

She laid a big dish on the table. The boilin' pot cleared a way through the crowd for itself, an' out tumbled a stew av rabbits an' bacon an' vegetables that would have tempted a sick millionaire, let alone a man on a diet.

'It's hardly done yet, but take that in your fingers, sir,' sez she, handin' him the leg av a rabbit, 'an' just pick it as you stand there. Now, take it! It won't talk to you — barrin' you prosecute my man for shootin' it accidentally in Mr Bermingham's demesne, an' a gentleman like you won't do that. Fetch the whiskey, Michael,' she shouts at her husband. 'I'll hold the twins. There's plenty more where that bottle came from,' sez she slippin' the twins' two two-shillin' bits into her husband's hand with a wink; 'but porter'll be better for you.'

Mr Anthony leaned over to me as he was standin' with a glass in one hand an' the leg av a rabbit in the other.

'Take this bone out av my mouth,' he mumbles. 'I've near swallowed it twice; an' it would be sure to go down with the whiskey. I can't refuse to eat with these poor people,' sez he. 'The Irish are very proud, and it would be taken as a deadly insult. And, curse it, I'm entitled to somethin' for my sixteen bob. By the way, did you see any sign av the turkey, or has it got lost in the stew?'

I shook my head as if I didn't hear him, for, troth, I'd been wonderin' about the turkey myself. An' when we were goin' out av the house, afther me an' Mr Anthony had drunk another couple av sups av whiskey an' Mr Anthony had bought two reserved tickets for a concern in aid av the new chapel, I drew Mrs O'Green behind the open cupboard door.

'What became av the turkey?' sez I.

'What turkey?' sez she. 'My man shot no turkey, or if he did it was an accident.'

'Mr Anthony is on a diet,' sez I in her ear; 'but had his Christmas dinner bought, an' sent you an' your family half av it, a turkey an' dear knows what besides. The housekeeper was to bring or send it, an' Mr Anthony came round hopin' for a wing or a leg, so that he could eat an' still keep his conscience clear.'

Mrs O'Green took a look at me, an' then a half-scared look over her shoulder at her husband.

'Come outside,' sez she. — 'It's that ould bitch av a housekeeper,' sez she. 'Oh, well I know where our turkey is gone. It's decoratin' the insides av her an' her two sticks av sisters that hasn't chick or child between them, an' me with five hungry children an' two I'm feedin' myself an' wouldn't have a bite in the house this day if my hard-workin' man hadn't shot three rabbits an' a water-hen yesterday evenin' an' him skulkin' behind hedge an' ditch to keep out av sight av the gamekeeper that's leatherin' into our turkey this minit — an' I wish he had shot *him,* too. But, for the love av mercy, Pat Murphy, say nothin' to nobody; for Michael has a wee sup av drink on him, this bein' Christmas mornin' — that was why I gave him the twins to hold; to keep him at peace — an' if he hears this news there'll be the siege av Athlone! Away with you,' sez she; 'for he has his eye on me, an' for all he's a good faithful husband he's wicked in drink, an' might do somebody a mischief if he found out. God send I'll be able to keep it from him an' save his soul from sin this holy day, an' me with a couple av mouthfuls av whiskey in me, too, an' long-tongued with it, that the like never crossed my lips since the two blessed twins were christened Aloysius an' Timothy by Father O'Leary in this very house an' them dyin' but lived since, an' we had half a pint av whiskey that isn't paid for yet, an' I hope that ould extortioner down the street won't keep Mr Anthony's two shillin'-bits again' it an' not let us have the porter.'

Mr Anthony was a temperate man, generally, more used to eatin' than drinkin'; an' when I caught up with him I found him two or three notes higher in the tune than when we left Williamson's, an' a little inclined to hiccough, though he handled it in a very gentlemanly way.

'There's a native courtesy about the Irish people, Pat,' sez he, 'a fine old standard av princely hospitality — *hmph!* I beg your pardon,' sez he. — 'Look at that poor creature with one miserable rabbit in a pot along with very bad company, and, damme, she was handing round legs av it as if it was a centipede. She wanted me to take whiskey, too. I wish I had. There's something sticking in my gizzard about half-way down, blast me but I think it's a claw. She should have cut the claws off, shouldn't she, Pat? No system about the Irish, all happy-go-lucky. Now I'm a me-methodicalman,' sez he, takin' it in a rush. 'It runs in my mind, — he stopped in the middle av the road an' began to grope in his pockets — 'that I've lost somethin'. — What do you think, Pat?'

'What do you think you've lost?' sez I.

He looked at me a bit wanderin' an' peevish.

'I don't *think* I've lost,' sez he. 'I know. — Wait till I think what it was. I have it,' sez he. 'What became av the turkey? An' if it comes to that ——' he looked at me all surprised, 'what became av the Limerick ham?'

An then the divil entered into me.

'Mr Anthony,' sez I, 'should we not call round by the gamekeeper's house? Your old housekeeper is sure to be there, an' she would take it as a great compliment.'

'So she would,' sez Mr Anthony, stoppin' in the middle av the road again, an' forgettin' all about the turkey an' the ham for the time. 'A very proper thing, too. Lord av the Manor visits old retainer — what? Lead on, Macduff. Wait a minute,' sez he, wrinklin' up his forehead as if he was still tryin' to remember somethin', 'do I look like a man that was on a strict diet?'

'You look like a man that will be on a quare strict diet tomorrow,' sez I.

An', sure enough, the whiskey was gettin' more av a hold av him every second.

'I don't mind about tomorrow,' sez he, devil-may-care all at once, 'so long as I'm all right today. And I don't care for any keeper — gatekeeper, gamekeeper, or housekeeper. If she opens her mouth to say the word "diet" — if I even see it in her eye — I'll give her a month's notice without the option av a fine. Come along!

'Wait a minute,' sez he again; an' this time he looked worrieder than ever. 'If we should meet Betty! *That* would be awkward, Pat. I couldn't give *her* a month's notice, could I?' He wagged his head very solemn as if there was nothing to be said for the opposite side. 'And she could give *me* notice on the spot. Hold on,' sez he. 'What day is this? Christmas Day. And she'll have had her lunch. She couldn't come out full av lunch on Christmas Day and sack poor Anthony that has nothing inside him at all — at any rate nothing that's doing him any good. No, no. Posterous. — I mean,' sez he, pickin' his steps through the syllables very carefully, '*Pre*-pos-terous.'

'Now, listen to me, Pat,' sez he when we got under way once more, 'we must do this in style. The old castle — the gamekeeper's house is the old castle. The wicked Baron — that's the housekeeper; and very wicked she was this day when she found I'd given away the family's dinner. The gallant knight — quite clearly that's G. Anthony, Esq., solicitor-at-law except on Christmas Day. And the beautiful damsel is Betty.'

'But she isn't here,' sez I.

'I know that,' sez he, shakin' his head very mournful. 'It's just as well.'

'An' where does Pat Murphy come in?' sez I, humourin' him.

'You don't come in at all,' sez he, 'if you have any sense. For, there's going to be bloody wars. Do you think,' sez he, lookin' at me as if he was an owl that had sat up playin' cards till night-time, 'that I didn't spot what that ould deceiver had done with my Christmas gifts? Well, I did *not* spot it. I'm a man that makes so few blunders that I can acknowledge when I do make wan. The whole way along I thought for a while it was my eyeglass. It was fluttering about me like a butterfly; but I caught it at last. And then all at once I saw that old harridan av a housekeeper carrying away my good dinner to her friends and leaving the poor and hungry with nothing to cover their nakedness but some d——d whiskey. Halt!' sez he, pulling up on his toes. 'We're at the gate. Form fours! Do you see that?' sez he, pullin' a wee tin-trumpet out av his pocket. 'The youngest walking O'Green child gave me that — and I'm still two and fourpence down over the transaction. When I blow three blasts on that — over the top!'

He blew three blasts on the wee trumpet — the first two were misfires — an' away up the path with me a good distance behind him — for the whiskey was beginnin' to die in me, an' I was feelin' a trifle ashamed av the whole transaction. When I got into the eatin'-room he was standin' at the head av the table holdin' a champagne bottle by the neck. The gamekeeper an' his wife, the lodge-keeper an' *his* wife, an' the house-keeper were all seated round such a spread as you never saw, bar in a picture — a turkey, a ham, plum puddin', cakes, sweets, bottles, an' glasses. They were just goin' to begin. There was a big salmon trout in front av the gamekeeper, an' he had dealt it all round the party an' given himself the ace.

Mr Anthony was lookin' down on them with what would have been a frown if his features could have kept their places in the class.

'It *is* my dinner,' sez he, catchin' a hiccough just as it was tryin' to escape. ''S *all* my dinner. That's my trout you're eating. You might think that's boiled trout; but it's not. It's poached trout. And I got a present av it because I proved to the satisfaction av a magistrate that it wasn't poached trout. So, *where are you?'* sez Mr Anthony so loud all av a sudden that the gamekeeper raised his knife an' fork to protect him self.

You never saw five people as willin' to be in another place as the party round that table. But the gamekeeper gathered himself together.

'You're wrong, sir,' sez he, very soothin', a thing that didn't help his case at all. 'I got this fish from Big Billy Lenahan av the Hills.'

'So did I,' sez Mr Anthony; an' the gamekeeper didn't know the answer.

'The fish was a present to me,' sez he at last. 'That it may choke me if it wasn't,' sez he, gettin' desperate.

'Very good,' sez Mr Anthony with great satisfaction. '*Let* it choke you. Stand up and swallow a mouthful; and if the fish doesn't choke you

I'll make it apologize.'

The gamekeeper looked at his wife most pitiful, but she had nothin' to say; an' Mr Anthony seemed very determined. So the gamekeeper stood on his feet with the plate av fish in one hand, balanced about a couple av ounces on the blade av his knife, an' made a shot at his mouth. He half caught the piece av fish, saw it was slippin', took a sudden suck; an' between that an' six pairs av eyes watchin' him, two av them in hope, sure enough he choked. An' the right name av it was chokin'. He was a short-necked, red-faced man when he started, but before you could count three he was purple, an' the eyes were comin' out av his head. I think it was his bad conscience more than the fish; but one or other looked like bein' the death av him. The three wimmin let a combined family yell an' gathered round him cryin' an' lamentin'; the brother-in-law got him under the arms; an' between pullin' an' haulin' they had him out av the room an' into the kitchen in a twinklin', an' the door shut. I didn't know till the next day whether he lived or died.

For Mr Anthony wasn't a bit put about, but laid down the bottle av champagne an' took up a whiskey-bottle.

'Seein' I'm on a diet, Pat', sez he, 'and have to deny myself, and you don't like champagne, we'd better begin the wake with whiskey.'

He poured out two tough ones; an' he had finished first.

'Now, Pat,' sez he, 'do you take the turkey an' I'll take the ham.'

But I was beginnin' to feel the weather a bit myself, now; an' somehow it didn't seem right that I should have the honour av carryin' the turkey.

'No, no, sir,' sez I. 'I take the ham.'

We didn't get it settled; for just as I spoke, a big boulder av a stone came flying through the window an' carried about a quarter av the plates an' glasses to their long home.

Mr Anthony seized the champagne-bottle again, an' dived under the table-cloth.

'Take cover,' sez he. 'He isn't dead yet.'

I got behind a chair, waitin' for the second bomb. An' as Mr Anthony poked his head out from the folds av the table-cloth, holdin' the champagne-bottle at the 'Present', in rushes Michael O'Green with his two eldest boys on his heels, an' him wild-lookin'. He didn't even hear the pop as Mr Anthony fired.

'Yez stole me Christmas dinner,' sez he, 'but yez'll never eat it.'

An' with that he lays hands on the turkey.

'Grab all you can lads,' sez he. 'What's not ours we'll make ours.'

But even in the state he was in by this time Mr Anthony was still the legal man.

'Justice and fair play,' sez he, risin' to his feet, with his thumb in the champagne-bottle, an' it thinkin' it was tryin' to put out a fire. 'Take what you like; but leave the ham.'

It was like a ghost risin' before Michael. He let half a prayer, half an apology, out av him, lifted the turkey, called off the family with what plunder they'd laid hands on, an' away down the road, gallopin'.

But nothin' could shake Mr Anthony by this time. 'You were quite right, Pat,' sez he as solemn as if he was on the Bench; 'you do take the ham. I'll carry the champagne, if I can get it to my head without being dhrowned. Fetch wan av those bottles av whiskey as well, or the battle av the Boyne will be fought over again in Creel's Row this day.'

He wasn't far out. Robert Williamson was a quiet determined man that liked to get to the bottom av things, an' insisted on what was his due. When he came home his wee son told him enough about the dinner he had missed for him to get the whole story out av his wife. He put on his hat.

'Leave the dinner till I come back,' sez he. 'I'll either have that ham with me or Michael O'Green by the hair av his head.'

When he got to O'Green's the family was just takin' their places in triumph for such a feed, between rabbit stew an' the turkey, as would go down in the family history for generations to come. Robert wasted no words.

'I see you have your turkey,' sez he to Michael. 'An' that old bigot av a housekeeper let you have our ham as well. If I don't get it in two minits, I'll kick the stuffin' out av you an' the turkey both.'

Any other time, Michael would have asked nothin' better than to let him try. But he had been greatly soothed by his victory about the turkey.

'Mr Anthony kept the ham, Robert,' sez he. 'As true as death I haven't got it.'

'Then I'll have the turkey,' sez Williamson, quite simple an' straightforward; lays hold av it by the legs, an' lifts it from the dish.

'Will you, by my sowl?' roars Michael, flamin' all at once, an' lays hold av the turkey by the neck; an' in a minute the two av them was pullin' tug-av-war all over the kitchen floor, with the family yellin' to raise the thatch. There was already a fair knot av Creel's Row people gathered since word had gone round about Michael O'Green arrivin' with a whole cooked turkey in his hand; so Mr Anthony an' I got through unbeknownst, an' into the kitchen just in time for Robert Williamson to miss Michael with the turkey an' hit Mr Anthony in the face. It was the first time I saw Mr Anthony real vexed the whole day. He brushed the loose bits av the turkey off his face, snatched the ham from me, an' liftin' it with his two hands felled Robert like a sheep. Then he came to himself again.

'There's your ham, Robert,' sez he in his ear, as Robert stood up half-dazed. 'I'm sorry it slipped out av my hand. But I'm on a diet; and a trifle weak with the hunger.'

The sergeant av polis had got wind av the turkey, an' came in with two constables just in time to prevent a European war; for Michael an' his family weren't too well pleased with the condition the turkey was in by this time, an' wanted to lay claim to the ham. But the trouble was settled, for the time bein', with the help av the bottle in my pocket. The sergeant sent Williamson an' the ham home under escort, an' volunteered to dhrive Mr Anthony an' me back in his own wee car; an' when we got there Mr Anthony got round him to fetch word to Mr Livingston's that Mr Anthony had been slightly injured while heroically separatin' two men engaged in a party fight, an' wouldn't be able to go for dinner.

As my head began to clear I could see that he was wrong.

'You'll have Miss Betty back here as sure as eggs are eggs,' sez I; 'an' where'll you be, then, with the state you're in?'

Mr Anthony looked at me, an' would have turned pale but for the gravy av the turkey that was crusted on his face.

'Curse it,' sez he, 'isn't it hellish the way a fine brain like mine is blunted by even the smell av drink. Come up to the bathroom with me, quick, and do you pour water on my head. I'd miss myself with Niagara Falls.'

I thawed the gravy off him with hot water, an' had got him into purty fair order with cold, when sure enough we heard wheels; an' the next minute Miss Betty was in the hall.

'He's puttin' on his dressin'-gown, Miss Betty,' sez I, runnin' out with a towel on my hand, 'an' will speak to you over the banisters. Don't let her within ten steps av the stairs av you,' sez I to Mr Anthony before he went out; 'for between wet an' dry that you've put into you this day your breath'll be like a pole-cat.'

So Mr Anthony perjured himself from the top av the stairs, an' made it all sound like sober truth, though it was neither; an' Miss Betty's eyes near lit up the stair-rods she was so proud av him for reddin' the party row when the polis couldn't do it.

'You'll be able to come to dinner,' sez she, coaxin'.

'I think I will, afther all,' sez Mr Anthony, never heedin' the kick I gave him. 'But, mind you, Betty, not even my injuries are to be an excuse for breaking the diet. I'm a man av my word should it snow turkeys.'

'Oh, *George*,' sez Miss Betty, 'how obstinate you are — and how dear.

I think I'll have to run up and kiss you.'

Mr Anthony cursed under his breath, an' took a very frightened skelly at me.

'Just a minute, darlin,' sez he, lettin' on to wrap the dressin'-gown tighter round him. 'Has Stubbs the chemist anything?' he whispers to me.

'He has capsules,' sez I, 'would make violets av a bad egg; but they take a while to work.'

'Betty, dear,' says Mr Anthony — 'it sounds very unromantic, I know — the truth is my lips are a good deal bruised. But Pat Murphy is getting me something from the chemist; and I think, darling' — his voice would have lubricated a stripped bearing — 'I think they'll be healed by dinner-time.'

Sealing Wax

It was no way safe to go out shootin' with Mr Anthony, at any time. When he took to the coortin' I made up my mind that the only chance I had av dyin' in my bed was to keep out av his way altogether.

But I still heard what he was doin'; an' he was at the coortin' strong. A mortal fine girl she was, too, Mr Livingston the new land agent's daughter, Miss Betty. It all begun with Mr Anthony takin' the office below Mr Livingston's, an' meetin' the daughter on the stairs. The first glimpse av her he got he tumbled over head an' ears in love with her; an' with the headstrong way he had av runnin' at everything he clean swept her off her feet. She was a pleasant-faced wee body, an' always the same whenever ye met her, an' had a pair av darlin' grey eyes with the kind av look in them that says 'Ye can depend on me.' To my mind she was just the girl for a twittery excitable wee body like Mr Anthony.

I'm not sayin' a word against the wee man, mind ye. A more open-handed wee fellow never stepped, or a kindlier, an' was as true as steel; but to live with him all his life was no nervous body's job. It was in my mind, anyway, to give him the go-by till he was married an' settled down an' had give up the shootin' for good.

I wasn't able to manage it, as things turned out.

It was all over a great hare that come to the Scroggy Knowe an' beat everybody to kill. Coortin' an' all, Mr Anthony heard about her, an' coortin' an' all, he be't to go afther her like the rest. By his own account, he didn't kill her less than five times in the first fortnight; but the only body he was able to produce was wan av Tammas McGorrian's yearlin' calves, an' people was av the opinion that as far as Mr Anthony was concerned the hare was still in the land av the livin'. But the last av the times he killed her he was so certain about it that he shook folks a bit. Less than half an ounce av lead he hadn't put into her, he swore, an' saw her rollin' over twice. He give in that when he got up to the spot she was gone; but it was only to go away somewhere to die, that he was positive about, an' left the gun behind him the next night he came out, an' went round searchin' the ditches with a pair av opera-glasses.

Wee Robbie Dixon told me about seein' Mr Anthony wanderin' round; an' when I heard he had no gun with him it come into my head that now was my time to have a shot at the hare myself, seein' that if I did meet Mr Anthony his fangs was drawn for one evenin'. So I took down the old muzzle-loader, put a couple av charges into her, an' off I starts for the Knowe.

When I got there I saw signs av either the hare or Mr Anthony, an' afther a while I got tired trapesin' about, an' made up my mind to save my powder an' shot, an' got off home. But that very minit a flock av green plover riz just across the hedge from me, an' I let off the two barrels at them. I seen a couple av them fall, an' was runnin' along the hedge lookin' for a gap, when I heard a great patterin' av feet behind me. I stopped an' looked round, makin' sure the polis had me this time, an' who was it but Mr Anthony, runnin' hot-foot, with the eyeglass bouncin' off his chest with every step, an' him trippin' over every briar-shoot an' whin along the ditch-side.

'Did ye kill her, Pat?' sez he, stutterin' with the excitement, an' glammin' all over the breast av his waistcoat for the glass. 'Is she dead? Where is she?'

'Did I kill who?' sez I.

'The hare,' sez he; 'was it not her ye shot? I've been trackin' her this half-hour, an' she came up this way. Half a dozen times I seen her,' sez he, 'an' got within fifty yards av her, creepin' on my hands an' knees. Look at my breeches. Av all the luck,' sez he. 'Fifty yards, did I say? Not thirty yards, either. I saw her as plain as I see you, sittin' up with her ears cocked. Damme, you'd think it was to spite me. Twenty years I might walk about this blasted hill with a gun in my hand, an' see nothin'; an' the first time I come out without wan I have to pick my steps for fear I'd tramp on a hare. — What did ye say ye shot, then?'

'A couple av green plover,' sez I.

'Ay, that's more av it,' sez Mr Anthony. 'Green plover?' sez he. 'They've been as thick as midges all evenin'. I had to brush them away from my face with my handkerchief. You'd think they knew I had no gun. An' I felt I could shoot this evenin', too. Was there ever such luck? — Here, Pat, lend me that ould musket av yours, an' we'll have a look round for the hare before we go home.'

'Ye won't do much harm with that, anyway,' thinks I to myself, handin' him the empty gun.

'I wonder ye wouldn't buy yourself a breech-loader,' sez he, looking at the gun a bit disgusted.

'If ye'd a wife an' six childer to keep, ye wouldn't wonder a bit,' sez I. 'She does my turn well enough. I wish I had all I ever killed with her.'

'I doubt I couldn't do myself justice with a weapon like this,' sez Mr Anthony. 'But away an' get the plover, an' we'll take a walk round.'

'Where did you see the hare last, Mr Anthony?' sez I, when I come back.

'She was sittin' in the corner av Mr Bermingham's ten-acre field, just waitin' for me to shoot her,' sez he. 'An' then that young thoroughbred av his — the wan his daughter is lookin' to win the Hunter's Cup with — came canterin' over the hill, an' the hare made off along the ditch, goin' easy. She'd settle down again very soon, if we could only tell where. Come on, Pat, we'll go round that way.'

'Sure it's fallin' dusk now, Mr Anthony,' sez I. 'You'd never see her.'

'Of course I'd see her,' sez he. 'That's the best av bein' a trifle short-sighted. I can see as well in the dusk as in the daylight.'

'An' that's the truth, anyway,' sez I to myself. 'But his claws is pretty well cut with the gun bein' empty.'

It was a blessin' she was empty. Every rush-bush an' tussock av grass he seen, down he'd go on his hunkers fixin' the glass tighter in his eye with wan hand an' waggin' the gun behind him with the other for me to make no noise. If there had been a couple av charges in the gun, or even wan, I wouldn't ha' been in my own shoes to get a pension, an' I wouldn't ha' dhrawn it for long if I had got it.

We wandered round the ditch av the ten-acre field this sort av a way, Mr Anthony every now an' then keekin' through the bushes, an' pluckin' the glass out av his eye on a thorn-branch every time he drew back his head. The third or fourth time he done it, crack goes the glass again the barrel av the gun an' into fifty pieces.

'Now we'll get goin' home,' thinks I. An', troth, I wasn't sorry; for my back was near broke with the stoopin'. But not a bit av it. Mr Anthony's blood was up, an' he wouldn't listen to me.

'Blethers,' sez he, 'I can see just as well without it. It's only a d——d nuisance, anyway. I shot a cock-pheasant a month ago, an' me had the wrong eye shut in my hurry. Easy here now, Pat; this is a likely corner. — Hush! Don't stir.'

Down he goes on his face in among the briers, as if shootin'-suits was got for nothin', an' pushes the muzzle av the gun through the hedge. I heard wan click, an' then another, an' then afther a minit out he comes, feet foremost, from among the briers.

'She's missed fire,' sez he in my ear. I could hear his teeth grindin'. 'D——n the ould blunderbuss, she's missed fire; an' I had the hare that well covered that I was near afraid to fire for fear av blowin' her to bits.'

'Sure the gun wasn't loaded, Mr Anthony,' sez I. 'Don't you mind? I fired the two barrels just before ye come runnin' up.'

I don't know whether a man can curse wickeder undher his breath or not, but it sounds wickeder.

'Couldn't ye remind me, ye thick-skulled old dundherhead,' sez he at last when he had his system brave an' well cleared. 'Did ye think it was a bird-av-paradise I was out afther, that I'd be satisfied with lookin' at it. Wait; maybe she's not away yet.'

Down he goes into the ditch again, an' comes out fair squirmin' with excitement.

'She's there yet,' he splutthers, 'damme, she's there yet, an' nearer the ditch now, if anythin'. Gimme your powder an' shot, quick!'

'I have no shot with me,' sez I. 'I just brought out the powder-horn in case the primin' fell.'

But if he was vexed before, he went fair demented then. What he had said at the first was nothin' to what he got out av him this time.

All at once he stopped.

'Hold on,' sez he; 'we're not beat yet. Gimme the powder.'

He snaps the powder-horn from my hand, an' with him bein' all av a tremble, I would say he didn't pour in less than a quarther av a pound into the left barrel.

'What's the good av that, Mr Anthony?' sez I. 'Ye'll never kill the hare with powder, barrin' she sits down on the muzzle.'

'Stones,' sez he, 'ye old fool,' glammin' all round him on the ground. 'Small stones. Search about you, there.'

'Not a bit av use, Mr Anthony,' sez I. 'Ye'd only blow them to dust, especially with the charge you have in. Sure there's enough powder in the gun to blast granite. You'd need to use metal av some kind.'

'Have you anythin' about you that would do, Pat?' sez he, feelin' all over his pockets. 'Confound it all, why did I change into my shootin' clothes. Ye haven't a pen-knife, or a key? Feel now, quick.'

'Nothin' but the key av the barn door,' sez I, fetching it out. 'An' the only thing ye could fire that out av would be a dhrain-pipe.'

'I've the key av the safe myself,' sez he, gropin' in his pockets; 'but I have to hand over the Maxwell deeds tomorrow, an' if the sale fell through I'd lose over two hundhred pounds av fees, an' me wantin' to make money just now. Tck, tck, tck,' sez he, 'was there ever such a spite? If I could only kill that hare I'd wipe the eye av the whole country. An' Betty wouldn't want me to stop shootin' then. Wait — wait now — I have somethin'.' He looks in the palm av his hand a minit, considherin' — 'No,' sez he, to himself, 'I daren't do it.'

Just then we hears a thumpin' av hoofs on the far side av the hill.

'It's that cursed horse,' sez Mr Anthony, dhroppin' somethin' in the gun an' leppin' into the ditch. 'The hare'll be away.'

'Take care, Mr Anthony,' I calls to him. 'Watch where ye shoot!'

But I was too late. Bang goes the gun like young thundher, with the charge was in her. Mr Anthony lights on his back among the briers with his heels in the air, an' the same minit there comes a terrible screech av a horse from across the ditch.

'Oh, Heavenly Powers,' sez I to myself, 'he's shot Mr Bermingham's thoroughbred!'

The wee man was crawlin' out from among the briers with a face the colour av chalk, barrin' wan bad tear av a brier across his nose.

'I doubt, Pat,' sez he, all shakin', 'I've done some harm to the horse.'

'Doubt be d——d,' sez I. 'Did ye not hear the scream av him? Listen a minit.'

We stood there gazin' at each other. But not a sound from across the hedge. I jumped into the ditch an' looked through. The horse was lyin' just on the crown av the hill, an' as well as I could see in the dusk there wasn't a move on him barrin' a bit av a twitch in his hind legs.

'He's killed dead,' sez I; 'an' what's to be done now?'

But for the first time in his life Mr Anthony had nothin' to say. He just stood there gapin' at me, with his knees shakin', an' every now an' then tryin' to put the string av his eyeglass in his eye as if the glass was still on the end av it.

'Come on, Mr Anthony,' sez I, stoopin' for my gun. 'There's no use cryin' over spilt milk. We'll put a mile or two between us an' this, anyway. Keep close along the ditches, for fear we'd be seen. Run now like blazes.'

Away we went, hell for leather, Mr Anthony leadin'; an' for the size av his legs it was wonderful how he covered the ground. When we'd run about a mile or so I called on him to stop; for he had me clean winded.

'We'll separate now, Mr Anthony,' sez I. 'Nobody seen me leavin' the house with the gun; I'll slip her back quietly now it's near dark. An' anybody that met you knows you came out av Ballygullion with a walkin' stick, so you're all right. Good-bye, now. You've got off better than you deserve, an' be thankful. Take to drink if ye like, from this on, but for Heaven's sake sign the pledge against shootin'.'

'What's wrong with my shootin'?' sez Mr Anthony. He was comin' to himself, now the worst fright was off him. 'I'll lay my head to a ha'penny the hare's lying dead in the field. I seldom miss a snap-shot like that. The seal must have gone out through her. I was a bit heavy-handed with the powder.'

'The *what* went through her?' sez I.

'The seal,' sez he. His jaw dhropped, an' he stood looking at me open mouthed.

'Pat,' sez he, at the last, 'we're ruined. No, *you're* not ruined. I can pay for the horse. But I've lost half my practice, an' the easiest half av it, too, an' my best girl, an' my whole chances in life. This is the end av my shootin'. I should have listened to Betty. I was the makin's av a good shot — she gave in to that, — but I'm unfortunate at it, bad scran to it I'm unfortunate. The divil fly away with that dirty steeple-chasin' brute, could he not stand at peace like a Christian an' eat grass, instead av makin' a travellin' circus av himself —'

'What in the name av patience is wrong now, Mr Anthony?' sez I. 'How will we be found out?'

'Listen, Pat,' sez he. 'You know I'm coortin' Miss Betty Livingston. Everybody knows it. The whole gossipin' town av Ballygullion knows it, all but her father, an' he might have knowed if he'd had a light on the stairs up to his office. We kept it from him because I wanted him to give me the estate business on my merits, now that old Johnston is likely to retire, an' not have people sayin', an' maybe himself among them, I was coortin' his daughter for it. So Betty an' I have been writin' an odd note to each other; an' she wasn't too sure av the post-office — they take a great interest in a love-affair in Ballygullion's post-office — an' she gave me an ould seal av her great-grandfather's to seal up any letters I might send her. It was that I put down the gun,' sez he, 'thinkin' it would surely stop in the hare's body. But it didn't; an' now it's stickin' in the carcase av that gallopin' wild Arab av the desert, an' I may leave the country.'

'Wait, now,' sez I, 'what was cut on the seal?'

'Betty had my monogram cut on it before she gave it me,' sez he. 'But I wouldn't care a fig for that. I got my head clerk to draw it for me, an' he's wan av them fancy penmen, so the divil himself couldn't read it. But Betty's father'll know the seal.'

'Could ye not get Miss Betty to square him?' sez I.

'Is it tell her I fired off her seal at a hare?' sez Mr Anthony. 'Have ye no gumption about girls at your time av life? An' for another thing she'd never let me fire another shot if she heard av this disaster, an' I might want to start again sometime. No,' sez he, 'we'll take our chance. Maybe they won't dig the seal out av him. There's some good-luck due to me afther this evening's work.'

'I wouldn't put too much dependence on that, Mr Anthony,' sez I. 'Ye've been lucky with the girl, an' that's as much luck as a man can expect in wan year. If Mr Bermingham doesn't ferret out who killed the horse it's a queer thing. I tell you he'll raise bloody wars, an' he'll be all the worse on account av the beast bein' Miss Mary's. She was desperate set on the horse, an' she'll not let this lie. You'd better find out the price av a ticket for America,' sez I — 'for two.'

But the extraordinary thing was that there was no row riz at all, afther the first outcry when the horse was found. I had a nice wee story made up av where I was that evenin', against the day the peelers would be out cross-questionin' me; but the divil a peeler came near the house, nor even round the country as far as I could hear, an' ye may guess I kept my ears open. I heard Miss Mary Bermingham cried very hearty when the horse was being buried in the demesne, an' had two av the hoofs cut off to have them mounted; an' the father came out one evenin' to see the place where he was killed, lookin' very wicked, they said; but afther that there was no word av them makin' a move, an' I begun to think Mr Anthony's luck had turned. As for himself, he was as elastic as an india-rubber ball, any time; an' when he wasn't found out straight away he put the whole business out av his mind.

The only thing that bothered myself much was the seal; an' it kept on botherin' me. It still ran in my mind that they'd never bury the horse without the wound bein' well examined; an' if they did I knowed there was trouble brewin', for all the quiet way things was goin' on. So I kept a bit wary, with some mind av a handy lie always in my cheek; an' it was just as well.

About a fortnight afther the horse was killed I was standin' in Ballygullion market, when who should come up but Miss Mary Bermingham. Not that there was much to wonder at in that, for I knowed her well with her comin' out our way huntin' many a time; an' she seldom passed me without biddin' me the time av day, or maybe a bit av a crack. But I took a tight grip av my tongue all the same an' lay very low. She stood a minit or two askin' me about the wife an' the family an' the prospects av a good winter's huntin', makin' all the time as if she was just goin' to pass on. All at once she pulls her hand out av her pocket.

'Did ye ever see that before, Pat?' sez she, holdin' it undher my nose. There was a big gold seal in the palm av it.

'I never did, Miss Mary,' sez I, well pleased to be startin' with the truth, anyway. 'There's not many country farmers carries them things at their watch-chains.'

She looked very hard at me, but I didn't move a muscle.

'I found it in the demesne the other day,' sez she. 'You didn't hear av anyone losin' such a thing?'

'I did not then, miss,' sez I. 'But if I do I'll tell him who has it.'

'No,' sez she. 'Tell me first. I'd like to have the pleasure av givin' it back. Don't forget, now, Pat. If you hear av anyone that has lost a seal, you're to be sure an' tell me before you tell the owner.'

'I'll not forget, Miss Mary,' sez I, as she went off with a nod an' a smile. 'Boys,' sez I to myself as I stood lookin' afther her, 'isn't the wimmin deep, too. I wonder has she been to Mr Anthony yet?'

But I was brave an' easy in my mind about him even if she had, for whether it was the lawyerin' or a natural gift, I knowed Mr Anthony could lie like a burial-card. All the same, I thought I'd have a word with him, just to put him on his guard, so when I had the pigs sold, away I goes round to his office. When I went in they told me he was in the estate office upstairs, an' sent me into the private room to wait.

A mighty queer kind av a private room it was for a solicitor to have. I'd seen it many a time before an' knowed what it was like, but afther what had happened I thought it would ha' been different this time; but it wasn't.

There was guns all over the place, a double-barrelled breech-loader in one corner an' another behind the door, an' a match-rifle over the mantelpiece, with a huntin'-crop crossed over it. Away in a corner was a glass case full av stuffed birds that Mr Anthony had persuaded himself by this time he had shot; an' all over the mantelpiece, an' even on his desk, was cartridges av every sort an' description, some empty an' some full. Lookin' at it all, you'd ha' said he was a great sportsman altogether, an', troth, accordin' to his gifts, so he was.

I hadn't right finished takin' stock till in he came, lookin' that worried that I made sure somethin' had cropped up about the horse in the meantime; for the last time I seen him he hadn't a care in the world, no more than if horses was vermin.

'What's up, Mr Anthony?' sez I. 'What has gone wrong with ye?'

He slapped a handful av deeds down on his desk an' upset an inkstand before he answered me.

'That's right,' sez he, 'pour yourself all over the place. Hit me when I'm down. Damme,' sez he, pullin' out his handkerchief an' moppin' up the ink, 'damme, but the very writin' utensils are down on me. What's up Pat? I'll tell ye what's up. The landlord av the estate is upstairs, an' the agent with him, an' they're settlin' whether I'm to get the law work av half a county, and have as good as made up their minds to give it to me. I'm a made man,' sez he, 'an' my income is goin' to be trebled.'

'It's a very poor imitation av bad news,' sez I. 'What's wrong about it?'

'Listen an' I'll tell you,' sez he. 'You an' me is old friends; an' I must tell somebody. Betty has fallen out with me.'

'What about, Mr Anthony dear,' sez I.

'I don't know what about,' sez he, risin' an' trampin' round the room. 'That's the exasperatin' part av it. It all begun about four or five days afther that horse met with the accident. Up till then all was goin' on as usual. I had two or three notes from her, an' met her every day on the stairs. All at once she stopped comin', an' she stopped writin'. I hadn't been writin' to her, for reasons av my own, but I wrote then, an' all the answer I got was my ring back, an' my letters, an' the divil a scrape av the pen then or since, though I've written to her twenty times. I called at the house, and' she wasn't at home, though I seen her through the dinin'-room window both times I went. An' when I meet her in the streets she just turns an' runs. I know somethin' about dogs, an' horses, an' guns — ye'll give in to that yourself, Pat. Well, I thought I knew somethin' about wimmin, too; but I was wrong.'

'Ye didn't give her any cause to fall out with ye that ye can think av?' sez I.

'None in the wide world, Pat,' sez he. 'I've been beatin' my brains about it till I'm that muddled I can hardly draft a lease, an' blast me if I can think av anythin' that even a woman could take offence at; an' I make part av my livin' out av unreasonable wimmin. I give in that I've been a bit extra civil to Miss Mary Bermingham latterly, seein' that I was lookin' out for the estate work; but Betty knew what I was afther. She couldn't be shirty about that.'

'I suppose not,' sez I; 'though, mind ye, ye were on ticklish ground. There's nothin' else ye can think av?'

'Not a thing,' sez he.

'She wouldn't be vexed about ye losin' the present she give ye?' sez I.

'What present?' sez he.

'The seal,' sez I.

The wee man broke into the first glimmer av a smile I'd seen on his face since I came in.

'I bamboozled her there, Pat,' sez he. 'I bamboozled her there. I sent to Belfast the next day an' had a new seal cut with just the same curlikews on it as the old wan, as far as Dixon here could remember them, an' I didn't write to her till I got it. It was pretty cute av me, Pat, eh? I haven't spent fifteen years at the law to no purpose,' sez he, forgettin' his troubles for a minit.

'I know where ye are now, Mr Anthony,' sez I. 'Ye've been too cute; that's all has been the matter with ye.' An' I told him what had passed between Miss Bermingham an' me that very afthernoon. 'Ye can put two an' two together, Mr Anthony. Miss Betty has seen Miss Bermingham with the seal an' thinks ye lost her present, an' was likely a bit vexed, but would ha' thought nothin' av it in a day or two; an' you must come along with your false seal, throwin' dust in her eyes instead av ownin' up like a man. Ye know what she is herself, as straight as a rule, an' ye can guess what she thinks av your cleverness. Mark my words, that's what it's all about.'

I expected Mr Anthony to be dancin' round the room, cursin' himself; for that was the way with him. He was always either up or down. But there were queer turns in him, too. All he does is sit down at the table very cool and collected an' lay a sheet av paper before him on the desk.

'Wait a second or two, Pat,' sez he, 'till I think.' He sat there cogitatin' for a long time. 'It seems to me,' sez he at the last, 'that this is wan av those very rare an' distressin' cases where it's goin' to be necessary to tell the truth. It's unprofessional, but it'll have to be done. I'll have to tell Betty about killin' the horse, that's clear. Not that I mind about that. It was the brute's own fault, as I'll explain to her. You can bear me out on that question, Pat?'

'Anythin' you say, Mr Anthony,' sez I, 'I'll swear to.'

'But the awkward thing about tellin' Betty is that she'll never rest till I confess it all to Mr Bermingham and his daughter. That's how Betty is built. She can't help it. It's a most exasperatin' thing about her, but that's why I think so much av her, all the same. Now as soon as Mr Bermingham knows I shot his horse — or his daughter's horse — I lose my chance av the estate business. An' if I lose the estate business, Betty's father'll never look at me for a son-in-law. Livin' above me here, he knows fairly well what my practice is worth without it; an' he's a man av big notions. — Ye see what must be done, Pat?'

'The divil a bit av me,' sez I. 'It seems to me ye're in a fix.'

'Betty must marry me before I confess to Mr Bermingham; that's all,' sez Mr Anthony. 'She'll do it, too, the darlin', I know she will. She's fond av me, Pat, damme, she's fond av me; an' she doesn't care a fig for money any more than I do myself. An' she'll be that delighted with me ownin' up to her about the seal an' the horse that she'll do anythin' to please me. Gimme my pen,' sez he, gettin' excited all at once. 'I'll write to her this very minit. Half a dozen lines'll do. She'll come down to hear the rest. — There's no time to be lost,' sez he, scribblin' away for dear life. 'Fetch the office-boy, Pat. — Where's my seal? Look on the desk,' sez he, strikin' a match.

'I wouldn't use that false seal again, if I was you, Mr Anthony,' sez I.

'Of course not,' sez Mr Anthony. 'I'm a thick-witted fool. Blast it, I've burnt my fingers! — What'll I use? Here, the end av this will do,' sez he, pickin' up a cartridge-case an' clappin' it on the blazin' wax.

'Stop, Mr Anthony,' I shouts. 'Stop!'

But the powder was quicker than me. There was a flash, an' a bang would ha' split your ears. Away goes I backwards over the chair on the broad av my back. The case av stuffed birds just missed my head by about six inches as it fell; but if it missed me, the ceiling didn't, for my head was singin' for days afther from the dunt I got on the skull with a bit av the plaster centre-piece.

But the time I was right come to myself the room was cleared av the whole town av Ballygullion but Mr Bermingham, Mr Livingston, an' Mr Anthony's head clerk that was givin' me water. When he seen I was better, the clerk went out, an' I riz to my feet an' looked over at Mr Anthony. The two gentlemen had got his head on a cushion where he was lyin' on the floor, an' was pourin' into him what water was left in the jug afther puttin' him out. The eyebrows was burned off him, an' part av the hair; an' as for his face, you'd ha' thought they had swept the chimley with it. Divil a thing he could do but gasp an' curse, though they were doin' their best between sips av water to get out av him what had happened. Then they turned to me, but for all I was a bit dazed I had my wits well enough about me to let on I hadn't, so they made nothin' av that.

In the middle av the cross-examination who should come runnin' into the room but Miss Betty, an' at her heels Miss Bermingham. Miss Betty was as white as a sheet. She never says a word, but dhrops on her knees beside Mr Anthony an' takes his head on her lap.

'We're ruined now,' thinks I. 'He'll blurt out the whole thing before them all, with the state he's in. An' that very minit here don't I see Miss Bermingham stoop down an' pick up the false seal off the floor. She took one look at it, an' one at Mr Anthony an' Miss Betty. The two gentlemen was lookin' at them purty hard already.

Mr Anthony was the first to speak.

'Stand back, everybody,' he gasps out. 'There's somethin' I want to say to Betty.'

So we all drew back, not knowin' whether it was his last dyin' speech an' confession or not; an' Mr Anthony draws down Miss Betty's head an' whispers to her a long time.

'It's not so bad,' sez I to myself. 'Even if Miss Mary has found us out, Mr Anthony has his blow in first with the sweetheart.'

I could see Miss Betty's face changin' as he spoke; an' when he stopped she was as red as fire.

'Then you didn't *give* it to her,' sez she, takin' a look across the room at Miss Mary; an' with that she bends down her head an' kisses Mr Anthony where she thought his mouth was likeliest to be, an' she made no bad shot at it.

Ye should have seen Mr Livingston's face. He half-opened his lips to speak; but Miss Mary was beforehand with him.

'Not a word, now, Mr Livingston,' sez she. 'This is a case av true love, as you might have seen long ago, if you hadn't been so — so busy lookin' afther my father's affairs,' she puts in, smilin'. 'You're goin' to give your consent; an' father, you're goin' to make Mr Anthony solicitor for the estate. Now there's no more to be said.'

Mr Bermingham looked at Mr Livingston, an' then the two av them shook their heads, half-laughin', an' looked at Miss Mary an' back at each other again.

'Come on, now,' sez Miss Mary, 'that's settled. I see Mr Anthony isn't goin' to die this time; an' we're not wanted here.'

The two men went out, an' Miss Mary was just goin' afther them when Mr Anthony lifts his head.

'Wait a minit, Miss Bermingham,' sez he. 'There's somethin' I must tell you.'

'I haven't time now,' sez Miss Mary. 'Come on, Pat.' An' off she goes afther her father.

I sat in the outside office tellin' lies to the clerks I suppose fifteen or twenty minits; an' there was no stir at all inside. But at last Miss Betty looks out av the door with a very black face an' beckons me in.

Mr Anthony was sittin' up in a chair smilin' like a Christy Minstrel. When he saw me he riz up an' holds out his hand.

'Congratulate me, Pat,' sez he. 'I'm goin' to be married this day six weeks. If I'd only this horse business off my mind I'd be the happiest man in the world.'

'More power to the two av ye,' sez I, afther a whoop just to relieve my feelin's. 'I'm a poor man, but it's a queer thing if I'm not first in with my present.'

But I wasn't. Just that minit there comes a knock on the door, an' in walks the office-boy with a brown-paper parcel.

'You're to open it at once, sir,' the messenger said.

'All right,' sez Mr Anthony. 'Ye needn't wait. — Open it Betty,' sez he.

She an' I took off the wrappin', an' here out on the desk tumbles a horse's hoof, mounted in silver, an' a wee note stuck on it with a pin.

Mr Anthony looked at me, an' me at him' an' if I was the foolishest lookin' av the two it was because Mr Anthony's face was black.

'Read the note, Betty,' sez he at last.

Miss Betty opened it an' read:

> 'Dear Mr Anthony and Betty,
> I think this pin-cushion will be your first present. It's a token of friendship and goodwill — *and a close tongue*. Good-luck.
> Mary Bermingham.'

'Isn't she a brick,' cries Miss Betty. 'Is it any wonder I was jealous av her?'

'She's more than a brick,' sez Mr Anthony. 'She's an angel. Betty, you must go this minit an' thank her — for me in particular. Tell her I owned up to you about the horse. I'd like her to know that — though, mind ye, it was all his own fault. An' — an' Betty,' sez he, 'ask her when he was found did she see any sign av a dead hare.'

A Wag Of a Tail

If the moon would have stayed at the full for say a fortnight when Mr Anthony the solicitor's apples was ripenin' in his new orchard, there's no doubt he'd have had a powerful gatherin'.

But the course av the moon ran along as usual. Everybody in the town was fully aware that Mr Anthony had such a crop for quantity an' quality as had never been seen in Ballygullion before; for he told them that himself some hundreds av times; an' the first real dark night afther the eatin' apples yellowed the whole children av the population sunk their religious an' political differences an' descended on the orchard like wasps on a wall av plums.

Mr Anthony sent his office-boy out on an errand for me the next mornin' askin' me to come to see him at once, an' when I got there he was in a very bad temper.

'I'll get a dog, Pat,' sez he, afther purifyin' his system av bad language for about ten minits. 'I can't use a gun on the little divils, but, blast me, I'll get a dog.'

'Dogs were never very lucky with you, Mr Anthony,' sez I.

'What the deuce do you mean?' sez he, flarin' up. 'I was never very lucky with dogs, if that's what you're drivin' at. If I've been cursed all my life with a collection av brainless rabbits with dogs' coats on them, am I to be blamed if I smartened them up now an' again with a pickle or two av shot? — Anyway, what I want this time is not a sportin' dog but a big quiet soft-mouthed animal, all wool an' bark, that wouldn't hurt a blind kitten. I'll train him to walk round the orchard all night — you know very well I can train anything with four legs an' a tail on it — an' whatever livin' he sees or hears he'll just bark at it till I come. — What do you think av that for an idea?' sez he, fixin' me very triumphant with his eyeglass.

'I think you'll need to buy the poor brute a few glycerine jujubes before you put him on sentry-go,' sez I. 'But if you want a quiet fool av a dog I may tell you Big Billy Lenahan av the Hills tried to sell me wan yesterday that he said was the very thing for a family man like myself.'

'Could I depend on him bein' quiet?' sez Mr Anthony, a bit dubious. 'I wouldn't put much confidence in the same Lenahan.'

'Billy told me the childer might pull the tail out av him an' he'd never look round,' sez I; 'an' Billy would never let an ould friend like me down, I'm sure.'

'Ay, but would he let *me* down?' sez Mr Anthony. 'I got him fined again lately for poachin'.'

'I'll tell you what I'll do, Mr Anthony,' sez I. 'I'll go up to Billy this afthernoon an' pick a dog for you myself, an' bring him down to you if I'm satisfied. — Now, not a word!' sez I. 'I'd do more than that for you anytime.'

An', troth, I did more for him this time, too, before all was finished.

When I told Billy I wanted the dog for Mr Anthony he turned over near as much bad language in five minits as Mr Anthony himself. But in the end he gave in to me.

'Seein' it's to oblige you, Pat,' sez he, 'I'll let him have a dog to suit his turn; not the wan I offered you, for he's sold, but a quiet biddable beast that wouldn't snap within two inches av a midge. All the same it's a sin to expose a kindly good animal to certain death from that handless little pettifogger.'

He opened the stable door, an' out came a sturdy lump av an Irish terrier.

'That's a tough-lookin' customer, Billy,' sez I, 'to be the lamb you say he is.'

'Lamb?' sez Billy. 'Why, man, a lamb would chase him for his life. — Tommy,' he calls to a ragged wee fellow that was hangin' about the upper end av the yard, 'are you in your bare feet?'

'No, Mr Lenahan,' answers the boy, 'I have my boots on.'

'Come down, then, an' kick this dog for me,' sez Billy.

The wee fellow walked down the yard all smiles, an' hit the dog a welt with the side av his foot. I laid hold av my stick, to save the child's life; but the dog just turned round an' licked the little rascal's hand, an' wagged every inch av him behind his fore-legs.

'Isn't that a Christian animal, now,' sez Billy. 'Would you like me to take a kick at him myself?'

If I'd thought there'd have been any chance av the dog liftin' about three-quarters av a pound out av the calf av Billy's leg I'd have said 'Yes'; but I took pity on the poor brute.

'Don't trouble, Billy,' sez I. 'If he didn't worry you on sight, he's too good for this world, as it is.'

But, lo an' behold you, when I brought the dog down to Mr Anthony, an' told him my story, he wasn't half-pleased.

'Not that I'd be ungrateful, Pat,' sez he; 'but blast it, I wanted a dog, not a jelly-fish. Never mind, though,' sez he, brightenin' up; 'you've seen the hand I've made av a dog before now, haven't you?'

I've buried what bits I could find av two or three av Mr Anthony's dogs in my time; but tellin' the truth is no way to be popular.

'You're a wonder with anythin' from a flea to an elephant, Mr Anthony,' sez I.

'Well, watch me this time,' sez he; 'for I'm goin' to astonish you. I've been readin' a book on modern dog-trainin', an', damme, it's more interestin' than case-law. — Did you ever hear av such a thing as a conditioned reflex?' sez he.

'I never did,' sez I; an' I was tellin' the God's truth this time.

'Well, it's like this,' sez Mr Anthony: 'if you ring a bell ten or twelve times, an' give a dog a piece av meat afther each ring, in the end his mouth will water at the sound av a bell. — Now presently I'm goin' to give the animal a sharp tap with my toe. An' what'll be the result?' sez he, screwin' in the eyeglass, an' lookin' at me very serious. 'In half an hour's time he'll hate the very look av a child, an' every time he sees one he'll gowl like the trumpet av a merry-go-round.'

'If ould Cruelty to Animals catches you at it,' sez I, 'you'll gowl yourself to the tune av forty shillin's an' costs. But I see your notion.'

'An' what do you think av it?' sez he.

'There's a man in Portnagree Asylum thinks his belly is made av glass,' sez I, 'an' he's sensible compared to you.'

'Have you half an hour to spare?' sez Mr Anthony, layin' hold av his hat.

'I have not,' sez I; 'but if you'll give me wan half-hour to spend on my own business, I'll come back an' waste another on you.'

When I came back he was waitin' for me.

'Off we go, now,' sez he; 'an' damme, I'll show you somethin'. — Come along, sir,' sez he to the dog; an' up the street goes the three av us.

The first lump av a lad we saw, Mr Anthony waited till he was just abreast av us, an' stirred up the dog pretty brisk with his toe. The dog looked round at Mr Anthony in an enquirin' sort av way, wagged his tail, a trifle half-hearted, as much as to say, 'I don't quite get you,' an' walked on.

Then all at once, as I looked at that big tough-lookin' brute behavin' like a hen, an' minded all I could mind about Big Billy Lenahan for twenty years, it come into my head that there was a catch somewhere. The next minit I knew what it was.

Comin' fresh out av Mr Anthony's we were naturally in the best part av the town, with all dwellin'-houses in the street, an' not a soul to be seen. An', as we walked along, down the front steps av Mrs Sides's house comes her wee spaniel dog an' waddles over very supercilious to have a sniff with Mr Anthony's terrier. About three seconds did the whole thing, includin' the growl. The terrier spent another second or two shakin' the body, but it was time wasted.

Mr Anthony's brains doesn't often move straight, but they move quick. The next thing I remember was watchin' the eyeglass bouncin' off his shoulder-blades as I followed him full-belt up the vennel into Market Street.

But he was still Mr Anthony.

'Did you see that sideways dive av mine?' he gasps to me, as we came to a stop in the street. 'Damme, I've known a blackbird do worse over a hedge.'

'Oh, the poor wee dog,' sez I.

'Blast the poor wee dog,' sez Mr Anthony. 'I collect the whole rents av the Sides' family, that's what I'm thinkin' about. — Home as quick as we can go. Reach me my eyeglass from behind me, an' do you look out for the dog, too. If he as much as wags the end hairs av his tail at me it'll cost me a hundhred a year.'

'He won't know us,' sez I. 'Go by him with your nose in the air. — You didn't give him anythin' to eat, I suppose?'

'Anythin' to eat, is it?' sez Mr Anthony. 'I gave him half a pound av steak that was meant for my own dinner. It was part av the system,' sez he, catchin' the look I gave him. 'No matter who else he fell out with he had to be friends with me.'

'We'd better climb over roofs on our way home, then,' sez I. 'However he was fed where he was stole from, he ate light enough at that Judas, Lenahan's; an' the very memory av half a pound av steak'll make him your friend till eternity.'

An' sure enough, when we got by roundabouts back to Mr Anthony's house the dog was standin' in front av the hall-door with the body av the wee spaniel in his mouth.

He just dhropped it in time to dodge the runnin' kick Mr Anthony made at him; an' by the time Mr Anthony had done hoppin' round with his toe in his hand the ould housekeeper was glowerin' out to see what young villain had threw a brick at the door. The dog wagged 'Thank-you' at her as polite as a human-bein', picked up the spaniel an' walked into the house as composed as if he was wan av the bearers at its funeral.

The divil a word said the housekeeper, but threw a look at Mr Anthony, that was peerin' up the road in his short-sighted way, then beckoned me over with a quick little jerk av her hand.

'Where did he shoot it?' sez she under her breath.

But I hadn't time to answer.

'Shut the door quick, Mrs Jackson,' sez Mr Anthony, all in a splutter. — 'Stand beside me, Pat, an' deny everythin'. Here's the sergeant comin' up the road.'

The sergeant walked straight over to us.

'I suppose you know av the tragic occurrence, sir?' sez he.

'Dear, dear,' sez Mr Anthony, all surprised. 'What is it? Anybody killed?'

'Worse than that,' sez the sergeant. 'Mrs Sides's spaniel dog has been assassinated by a baste av an Irish terrier. An' hearin' you had been observed to have an Irish terrier in your immediate vicinity as you walked down the street some twenty minits ago I took the liberty av comin' up to interrogate you.'

'There may have been an Irish terrier followin' me, for all I know,' sez Mr Anthony, 'an' he may have chewed the spout off the town-pump for all I care; but he had nothin' to do with me. It's two years since I had an Irish terrier.'

'I mind that fellow,' sez the sergeant. 'You killed him in the bog beyond Drumcree.'

'He had the mange,' put in Mr Anthony, very hasty.

'Whatever he had you cured him av it, anyway,' sez the sergeant. 'If that was your last terrier you're dismissed without a stain on your character. An' it's just as well for you,' sez he with a very weighty nod av his head.

'Is she very angry?' sez Mr Anthony.

'Hellish,' sez the sergeant. 'I've seen less fuss made av an only child. She came down her own steps, roarin' like a female bull, an' offered me a twenty pound reward if I discovered the depredator. — Do you think, now,' sez the sergeant, 'if I went through the descriptions av the licensed dogs av this district I'd be likely to get a clue?'

'It's a great notion,' sez Mr Anthony. 'Don't waste a minit. Damme sergeant, if I had your brains I'd die on the Woolsack. — Did you mark that,' sez he to me, pullin' out his latchkey. 'Did you see how I set him off on a wrong scent just with a hint? — Come in, Pat,' sez he, in great twist with himself, 'come in an' celebrate my escape. — Here! here!' goin' to the door, an' whistlin'. He lifted a couple av biscuits from the sideboard an' threw them to the terrier.

'To Jericho with these yappin' little abortions,' sez he. 'No wonder he extinguished the little pismire. — Confound me but I like this dog.'

But when I called back in a couple av days' time to hear if all was still well he was singin' a different tune. He opened to me himself, an' as I looked down the hall I seen that the stained-glass fanlight over the door into the garden was all chattered-up.

'Had you a wee storm all to yourself, Mr Anthony?' sez I.

'Oh, that's nothin',' sez he, hurryin' me into the dinin'-room; 'just a triflin' accident as I was makin' ready to shoot the dog.'

'But I thought you had taken a fancy to him?' sez I starin'.

An' then Mr Anthony cast loose.

'A fancy to him!' sez he, when he came back to Christian expressions again. 'Is it take a fancy to that Jack the Ripper? Look at that bed.'

I looked; an' there was a big square flower-bed with the whole flowers gone, an' it all heaped-up an' out av shape.

'If you buried the dog there,' sez I, 'he must have swelled.'

'If I buried the divil!' splutters Mr Anthony. 'I buried three dogs there these last two days. That beast killed them all, an', blast him, fetched them back here as well. — An' that's not the worst av it,' he goes on groanin'. 'It's all my best clients in the neighbourhood that have been sufferin'. — Curse the brute, you'd think he read the daily paper, an' went straight out an' killed a dog av somebody he saw I was actin' for.'

'So you shot him?' sez I.

'That's the most exasperatin' part av the whole business,' sez he, beginnin' to stamp up an' down. 'The housekeeper wouldn't let me. — It's the dog himself. He's got round her,' sez he, shuttin' the dinin'-room door. 'Pat,' sez he, 'if I wasn't in the twentieth century, an' a solicitor at that, I'd say he was a witch, the way he humbugged an' bamboozled her. Right from the start he behaved like a gentleman, biddable an' clean an' good-natured. It's a miracle he didn't get cramp in his tail he was that grateful for any bite she threw him; an' one day she gave him the drumstick av a chicken he wagged five custard-cups off a tray. —But it was through the kitten he got really at her. She had a wee yellow kitten that was just the apple av her eye ——'

'Did you say *had*, Mr Anthony?' I puts in.

'I did,' sez Mr Anthony, a trifle short. 'Do you think I passed my law examinations without learnin' grammar? — Well,' he goes on, 'the brute made up to that kitten as if he loved it, carried it round by the scruff av the neck as careful as if it was made av china, an', damme, even drank milk out av the same saucer. — I'll give in he got the lion's share av the milk, but I don't believe that was why he did it. — You'll laugh at me, Pat, but I declare to you there's times when I believe there's a soft dhrop in that dog afther all. I've been readin' that psychology book av mine again, an', confound me, if there was any way av suggestin' to him that it was a bad thing to kill toy dogs I believe he could be cured av it. — However, in the end he put himself out av court altogether.'

'I can guess it,' sez I. 'He ate the kitten.'

'What the divil are you harpin' on the kitten for?' sez Mr Anthony very peevish. 'That wasn't it at all. — When he brought home Major Henderson's Peke he dhropped him in the stock-pot; an' afther that the housekeeper swore if I didn't shoot him she'd slaughter him herself with the cleaver. To escape notice I thought I'd do the job inside the house, so I lined up the dog at the end av the passage with two bags av coal behind him to catch any stray shot, an' tied a handkerchief over his eyes. — Damme,' sez Mr Anthony, warmin' up, 'it was just like the execution av Marshal Ney.

'The divil av it was that the brute wouldn't act up to the spirit av the thing, but still kept pullin' off the handkerchief with his paws. So I got the housekeeper to throw him a bone; an' as she stepped behind me with her hands to her ears, here doesn't she open her eyes for a second, an' if the dog wasn't waggin' his tail to say "Thank-you"!

'"Aw, the poor brute," sez she, an' glammed at my arm. Up went the muzzle av the gun, an' out went the fanlight. The dog made for the kitchen. I took a snapshot at him with the second barrel, an' had him as good as killed, when confound me if the little fool av a kitten didn't come prancin' out av the kitchen with its tail up, an' get in the way av the charge. — What are you snortin' at, you big booby?' sez he. 'Haven't you seen me many a time shootin' a rabbit between wan hole in a warren an' another?'

'Twenty times, Mr Anthony,' sez I, wipin' my eyes; 'but this is funnier. — Has she give notice?' sez I, noddin' my head towards the kitchen.

'No, confound the old hag,' sez Mr Anthony, very savage. 'She hasn't even that much respect for me. — She had the d——d impudence to tell me that if I'd aimed at the kitten I'd have killed the dog. — But no matter. He'll be dead very soon now.'

'Dead,' sez I. 'I'll never believe it till I see this corpse.'

'I poisoned a slice av bread an' butter with strychnine, an' left it in the orchard,' sez he, 'an' turned the dog out there just before you came. — Oh, my heavens!' he cries, lookin' out av the window, an' clapped his hand to his head. 'Mrs Jackson!' he yells, tearin' the door open. Up the stairs he dashes, an' down them in two lepps with a wee bottle in his hand. 'Come on, Pat,' he shouts, as he made for the garden door; 'come on, quick or we're too late!'

'What is it?' sez I, as I run. 'What *is* it, Mr Anthony?'

'Hippo-wine,' he calls back, raisin' the hand with the bottle. 'It's all I could think av. Oh, come on, Pat, come on.'

'He's for savin' the dog's life afther all!' flashes through my mind.

An' as he opened the orchard gate here were a couple av young lads under a tree, an' the wee wan av the two had an apple in one hand an' was just takin' a bite out av a slice av bread he had in the other.

The screech Mr Anthony let out av him wouldn't have disgraced an express-train.

'Stop, boy,' he shouts. 'Drop it! Don't move! — Oh, why didn't I kill that dirty brute with a hatchet!' sez he, lamentin' as he ran.

Now, as I need hardly tell you, stoppin' was the last thing in the children's mind. They didn't as much as squeal, but just took to their heels an' were out av sight among the trees before you could clap your hands.

'Run, Pat, run,' gasps Mr Anthony. 'Keep them goin'. The wee fellow has a bite in his mouth, an' another swallow might hang me!'

But on account av the trees I couldn't pass Mr Anthony; an' he was makin' no speed himself; for I suppose he must have pulled about a quarter av a stone av apples with his eyeglass before the string broke.

'There they are,' he gasps, as he broke through the hedge afther the pair, 'makin' for the labourers' cottages. We'll be up on the young fellow before he reaches them. If you're ahead just prise his mouth open, an' I'll have the stuff in him before he knows he's poisoned.'

'Wherever he's poisoned,' I pants afther him, 'it's not in the legs. He'll beat us to the cottages yet. An' if he drinks water afther the strychnine he'll just split open.'

Mr Anthony let somethin' out av him between a groan an' a squeal, spurted fifteen or twenty yards ahead av me, an' kept his lead all the way up the hill. Even with that the wee fellow beat him to the cottages, an' disappeared round the first wan. Mr Anthony let another whillaloo out av him an' spurted again. When I turned the corner here he had the young lad by the nose an' was jerkin' the contents av the bottle into him between yells. The last mouthful near choked the wee fellow, an' he was half up the steps av the next house before he got back his breath; but he made up for it, for the howl he let out av him as he entered the door was enough to loosen all the slates in the roof.

By this time there was a head out av every door an' window in the whole row, an' the next minit down the steps comes a big red-faced grenadier av a woman an' her with a yard-brush in her hand. She made one rush at Mr Anthony, an' started to flail at him with the brush as if she was threshin' corn, all the time keepin' up a string av abuse as well as her breath would let her.

'I'll teach ye — ye dirty little pup — my harmless wee fellow — assaultin' an' poisonin' an innocent boy —'

While this was goin' on, between the effects av the run, an' tryin' to dodge the brush, Mr Anthony could only get stray words out, on his part. He began polite enough in spite av his flurry.

'Madam — Madam — pardon me —' Here he made a glam at his hat to lift it, but the yard-brush saved him the bother. 'Let me explain — a minute —'

But with that the woman changed her tactics, an' gave him the point, as the sodgers would say. The bristles took him somethin' wicked in the face; an' when he got them down his nose an' out av his mouth he let wan yell av fury, pulled hard on the brush an' then pushed from him. The big woman sat down on the sidewalk an' stopped talkin' as if her head had fell off. She wouldn't have had much chance anyway.

'Confound an' blast you for an ignorant faggot,' sez Mr Anthony, dancin' round her fair stutterin' with the rage, 'I didn't poison your brat. He's just afther poisonin' himself with strychnine laid in my orchard — where he was stealin' apples, if you want to know —'

By this time the big red-faced woman was on her hands an knees gettin' up, an' the breath comin' into her again. She riz up about two feet above Mr Anthony, an' just guldhered at him.

'Stealin' apples?' she roars. 'My good well-behaved boy, that's only this minit gone down my steps afther eatin' his dinner —'

She got no further. A little pale woman on the edge av the crowd let a screech out av her, an' begun clappin' her hands an' callin' out.

'It's my son, it's my wee son. That dirty big loafer av Paddy Finnegan's tempted the poor angel down to the orchard, an' now he's lyin' dead an' buried in his own parlour under the sofa. Ah-h!' She let a yell about ten sizes too big for her, an' up the steps av the next house like an india-rubber ball.

'My G—d,' sez Mr Anthony. 'I've dosed the wrong child!' He pulled the bottle out av his pocket, held it to the light, an' up the steps afther the wee woman, an' me afther him.

The little pale woman was down on her knees beside the sofa, an' had hold av the child's leg, that was stickin' out from underneath. The tears was runnin' down her nose.

'Come out, darlin', quick,' she speaks undher the sofa. — 'Somebody run for the doctor,' she calls over her shoulder. — 'Let go the leg av the sofa, ye little wasp,' sez she, gettin' angry all at once, 'or I'll pull the foot off ye!'

Out comes the lad with a jerk, an' as the mother lifted him to his feet I seen he had a wee fragment av bread still in his hand. I jumped to snap it from him, but Mr Anthony grabbed it first.

'What this?' sez he, with the eyes gogglin' in his head. 'There was no jam on *my* bread.'

'That's none av your bread,' sez the wee woman. 'It's off my own good currant loaf, an' this wee heart-scald has jam on it, forbye. — Gimme my switch,' sez she, leppin' round the room like a tiger, 'an' if I don't warm his hide for the fright he's give us all this day!'

I pulled Mr Anthony by the tail av his coat, an' we shoved our way through the people that was crowdin' in, an' took to our heels for home.

'That's a sensible little woman, the small body,' sez Mr Anthony, when we'd got our breath a bit. 'Did you mark how easily I persuaded her that her boy was in the wrong, an' deserved all he got? But that big pig-faced feather-bed with the yard-brush is a danger. She's venomous, that wan. If some unscrupulous lawyer gets hold av her she may run me into a lot av money yet. — Come on,' sez he, very savage, pushin' all av himself but wan av the side-pockets av his coat through the hole in the orchard hedge; 'my luck must turn sometime. Maybe that old bitch av a housekeeper has poisoned herself.'

But not even the dog had done that. As we walked along the main path who should come to meet us but himself with the piece av bread very gingerly in his mouth. He laid it down at Mr Anthony's feet an' looked up in his face as much as to say, 'Now, there's a nice wee tit-bit I've been keepin' for you.'

'Ah, the poor fellow!' sez I. 'You couldn't find it in your heart to be angry with him afther that, now could you?'

But Mr Anthony was long past bein' got round that way.

'Could I not?' sez he, glowerin' at the dog. 'I know you,' sez he, 'you two-faced assassin. You want to see me kickin' on the ground in convulsions, an' you trottin' round me waggin' your tail with your tongue in your cheek. Drop it!' sez he, as the dog took up the piece av bread in his mouth again. 'I'll give you an easier death than that; but there's not room for both you an' me in the legal profession in this town. — I'll tell you what, Pat. Come up with me tonight to the water-works an' we'll dhrop him quietly in with a stone round his neck.'

'Lord bless us, Mr Anthony,' sez I, 'do you want the town to get typhoid an' us penal-servitude?'

'Oh, curse him,' sez Mr Anthony in a rage. 'I'd be happier with typhoid. — Wait,' sez he: 'couldn't we throw him in the overflow pool.'

'I suppose we could,' sez I, 'so long as he doesn't come up later.'

'Leave that to me, Pat,' sez Mr Anthony, all himself again. 'I'll lay my mind to the job this afthernoon with a ready-reckoner, an' calculate to a grain the exact weight av a stone that'll sink the beast nice an' quietly, an' keep him down; an' about nine o'clock to-night he'll pass out av this wicked world without as much as a ripple.'

When I got round to Mr Anthony's at a quarter to nine he fetched me out to the yard on my tip-toes. In the glimmer from the kitchen window I could make out a big square basket with a lid an' a handle.

'That's the dog,' sez he. 'We can carry him time about.'

'Is he paralysed in the legs?' sez I, 'or is he just too upsettin' to walk?'

'Are you paralysed in your brains?' sez Mr Anthony. 'Wasn't he near traced to my house already?'

'Oh, come on, then,' sez I. 'If this job went by common sense it's him would be dhrowndin' us. — What's that?' sez I, jumpin', as there come a crack from the basket.

'Nothin',' sez Mr Anthony. 'Only the bones av a chicken I gave the dog to keep him quiet.'

'Quiet,' sez I. 'You'd think he was sendin' off fireworks. The half av the town'll be at our heels before we're there.'

But we got to the waterworks unbeknownst, so far as I could make out, an' when we climbed over the palin's, if Mr Anthony didn't pull a flash-lamp out av his pocket!

'Put that out!' I snaps at him. 'Do you *want* us to be catched?'

But Mr Anthony, as usual, was an obstinate as a he-ass.

'In my readin' av the great Napoleon's campaigns,' sez he, 'one thing I learned was to make sure av my ground. — This is the town reservoir on our left. Do you see that swirl there? That's the outlet pipe. If we dhropped the dog into that the first place he'd stop would be at the polis barrack.'

'It's the first place we'll stop, too,' sez I, 'if you don't switch out that light. Feel round an' get a stone. The overflow pond is on your front. Don't forget that we're keepin' it for the dog.'

Away goes Mr Anthony wanderin' an' gropin' on his hands and knees for a stone; an' the next minit I felt a touch on my arm.

'All right, Pat,' sez Billy Lenahan's voice, in a half-whisper. 'Come back into your skin again. It's only me. Is this the dog you've got?' sez he, liftin' the basket. 'I heard him crackin' nuts as you went past me at the fair-green.'

'You can have him back, you big sharper,' sez I, 'if you'll tell me where he learned his bad habits.'

'There's no great mystery about that,' sez Billy. 'An' I'm safer without him, thank you. Colonel Fitzgerald fell out with his wife about her wee dogs, an' trained this fellow to kill them; an' then he fell in with her again an' gave me a couple av quid to put him out av the road. Since then, as you know, Mr Anthony paid me a pound for him; an' now you're puttin' him out av the way for nothin'. I'll go off an' look for another dog,' sez he; 'I done so well out av this wan.' An' away he slips into the darkness.

'Are you there, Pat?' calls Mr Anthony's voice in a minit or two. — '*Hell!*' sez he, as there came a crash, 'what did you move the basket for? — Will that do?' sez he, showin' me a stone with the flashlight.

'It'll do well,' sez I. 'Lend me a glimmer till I tie it on him.'

He picked up the dog, hit himself a most lamentable dunt on his knee with the stone, an' started to hop round on one foot.

'For heaven's sake look out,' sez I. 'If you dhrop him in the reservoir we're destroyed.'

'It's all right,' sez Mr Anthony, an' I knowed by his voice he was keepin' in some terrible observations. 'I was just takin' my bearin's.'

He hirpled on for a yard or two, an' then he stopped.

'Pat,' sez he. 'I left my calculations at home; but this stone is far too light. It should be seven pounds and a half, an' it's not that.'

'It'll do,' sez I, fair dancin' with impatience. 'You've been signalin' for the polis all night, an' they'll be here any minit. — Dhrown yourself or dhrown the dog; but for heaven's sake do it quick!'

'I can do better,' sez Mr Anthony; an' I knowed by the tone av his voice I needn't contradict him. 'The slope av the reservoir is paved with big stones. Take him by the scruff, an' do you show me a light with this thing till I find a loose one. The brute has tormented me for three days; I'll likely be in the Courts over him; an' now, blast him, he's broken my knee-cap. If he's goin' to the bottom, damme, he's stayin' at the bottom.'

'Go slow, then, Mr Anthony,' I calls, as soft as I could. 'You're in your own light. — Oh, my father!' sez I, as there came a most lamentable splash, 'he's in!'

The dog gave a wriggle undher my hand at the noise, an' twitched his neck out av my fingers. I caught a glimpse av him tearin' for the reservoir with the stone trundlin' behind him, an' the next minit he was in afther Mr Anthony.

By the time I got to the edge, Mr Anthony was out, an' crawlin' up the slope on his hands an' knees. As soon as I seen he wasn't too bad I left him on the grass to curse himself dry, an' showed a light on the reservoir for a minit. But there was no sign av the dog.

'Oh, Mr Anthony,' sez I — an' I declare to you I was half-cryin' — 'the poor brute jumped in to save you, an' now he's dhrowned.'

'I don't care he was in hell,' sez Mr Anthony. 'I expect he was tryin' to knock my brains out with the stone. An' now he'll be up again in three or four days floatin' round the town reservoir an' barkin' for the polis. — Come on out av this, d—n you, before I get my death!'

I never saw Mr Anthony so wicked in my life before. All the way back he never said a word, an' when we got to his house he didn't even ask me for a drink, but slammed the door in my face.

As I turned the corner av his house there came a wee cautious whistle; an' when I crossed the road it was Billy Lenahan.

'Well, I'll be hanged,' sez I, lookin' down at his feet.

'Oh, it's him, all right,' sez Billy, leanin' down to pat the brute. 'The stone came off him an' he swam out just beside me. You might have heard me callin' him quietly by name.'

'But I thought you didn't want him,' sez I.

'Ach, you could never tell,' sez Billy. 'A dog's a dog. Some av these nights one av Mrs Fitzgerald's wee atomies may bite the Colonel's feet in bed again, an' I'll make money on this fellow for the third time.'

'Well, I'm not sorry, anyway,' sez I. — 'Shake a paw,' sez I to the dog. 'You're in bad company, an' I doubt you'll come to a poor end; but, dammit, I wish you well.'

He put out his paw to me, hearty enough; an' as far as I could judge by the creature's tail we parted without any ill-will on his side, either.